SACRED SALT

A THRILLER

SACRED SALT

GODFREY CLARK BURNS, M.D.

Sacred Salt: A Thriller
©2021 Godfrey Clark Burns, M.D.

ISBN: 978-1-943190-26-3 (print)
978-1-943190-27-0 (eversion)

All rights reserved worldwide. No part of this publication may be reproduced, distributed, or transmitted in any form or by any means, electronic or mechanical, including photocopy, recording, or any information storage and retrieval system, without written permission from the author except in the case of brief quotations, embodied in critical reviews and certain other noncommercial uses permitted by copyright law.

Publisher's Cataloging-in-Publication data

Names: Burns, Godfrey Clark, author.
Title: Sacred salt : a thriller / Godfrey Clark Burns, M.D.
Description: Yachats, OR: Wild Ginger Press, 2021.
Identifiers: LCCN: 2021910279 | ISBN: 978-1-943190-26-3 (paperback) | 978-1-943190-27-0 (ebook)
Subjects: LCSH Murder--Fiction. | Murderers--Fiction. | College teachers--Fiction. | Physicians--Fiction. | African Americans--Fiction. | New York (N.Y.)--Fiction. | Mystery fiction. | BISAC FICTION / Mystery & Detective / General | FICTION / Thrillers / General
Classification: LCC PS3602.U76635 S23 2021 | DDC 813.6--dc23

Wild Ginger Press
www.wildgingerpress.com
Book & Cover Design by Bobbi Benson

TO
Joseph Salvatore and Russell Morse
Thank You

Salt is the only rock

directly consumed by man.

It corrodes but preserves, desiccates but is

wrested from the water. It has fascinated man

for thousands of years not only as a substance

he prized . . . but also as a generator

of poetic and mythic meaning.

The contradictions it embodies

only intensify its power and

its links with experience

of the sacred.

~ MARGARET VISSER

Prologue

For the flesh, if not sprinkled with salt, putrefies and is filled with a great stench; and worms crawl in the rotten flesh, and are nourished by feeding on it and lie hidden in its caverns.

– MACARIUS

HE TURNED THE BROWN BOTTLE on its side, and three tablets fell to the table. If his calculations were correct, these would replenish what had leaked from him since morning. He placed the tablets in the center of his raw tongue, avoiding its tender edges, then brought the glass of water to his lips. Rupert closed his eyes and swallowed.

It was July, with rain and gusts of winds since morning. A strong breeze shook the loose windowpane behind him, and a sudden flash of lightning scattered crooked shadows across his darkened room. Thunder followed—this time close.

He rested the glass on the table next to his bed and walked across the room to check his valise. All was there, yet he lingered, reaching inside to fondle the precious contents. Again, he closed his eyes, listening to the Voice in his head recite from Psalm 107:34: *Rivers were turned into deserts, and springs of water into a parched ground, and the fruitful land to a salt marsh, because of the wickedness of those who dwell therein.*

He stood on Twelfth Street, across from her building, disliking even the place where she lived. The darkened entrance and the absence of a doorman were welcomed blessings. He pressed the downstairs bell, and she buzzed him in. He walked close to the wall, head down, in case there was a camera. At her door, just before knocking, the Voice whispered, *Look at what nature has done to you.* A wave of nausea passed through him, and his heart quickened. He paused, then realized he'd miscalculated earlier: three tablets had been too many. Now his saliva was thick and sticky, making his mouth dry and even more painful. He gently moved his tongue across his front teeth, trying and failing to make saliva.

He knocked.

Margaret stood before him in a blue silk robe, a lit cigarette in her left hand. According to her hospital chart, she was sixty. He distinctly recalled the doctor's warnings against smoking.

Her blue eye shadow—too heavy—and lipstick—a garish pink—were carelessly applied. Her features were puffier than he remembered. He wondered: *Is this her disease, or has she been sleeping?*

"You're late," she said, pointing directly to the chair she'd chosen for him to occupy. At their first meeting in the hospital, she'd also demeaningly rebuked him through that tightened jaw; he remembered her saying, "Are you in charge of this floor? Get me a different room and do it quickly. This sunlight will kill me." And after Rupert did, she still registered that stupid complaint. Later, when he went through her records, he found other malicious grumblings from her previous hospital stays.

He stepped into her apartment and sat. The living room was small: sofa and rug off-shades of green, matching gold chairs, a coffee table, a mirror, one window, and no pictures. Tidy. But the smell of nicotine was sickening. *Doesn't she ever open the window?*

She'd set a tray of tea and cookies on the coffee table. When he'd called earlier, she'd been irritated and had pressed him on the progress of her complaint. "I can stop by and explain the details." Now, Rupert was there.

"Tea?" she offered without a smile.

"Yes, thank you." His voice was calm. *That's good.* Rupert folded his hands and tilted his head to the side, hoping she hadn't noticed his right leg trembling; he could feel the moisture in his armpits. But she was watching him—he knew it, could feel it—a half smile on her hardened face, enjoying every second of his unease.

"Well?" she said, opening her arms theatrically, demanding that he speak.

He moved his burning tongue under his lips to moisten his mouth. "As we discussed, the room in question has been fixed to address your complaint. Tinted shades have been added to deal with the glare."

She leaned back and smiled, passing a hand over her neck, reminding him of Bette Davis in *All About Eve.*

"The sunlight in that room devastated my skin and forced me to buy a lotion to restore its softness." Pointing a finger, she moved closer to him. "I came to the hospital for my heart—not to ruin my skin."

"We can reimburse you for the lotion."

"You can?" She smiled. "I've packed the receipt away; I'll get it now."

When Margaret left her chair, his scalp tightened, the vessels in his neck began to throb, and the thumping in his ears became louder. He took a deep breath to block out the sound.

He quickly removed the vial from his breast pocket and poured the contents into her cup. In the distance, a gentle thunder rumbled.

She returned to the room, placed an envelope on the coffee table, and sat erect. He followed her eyes as she took her first sip of tea. A slight frown passed across her face, and then she spoke.

"My complaint was justified." She raised her chin and stared at him. Her lipstick had stained the delicate white teacup. Her arm and the back of her hand holding the cup were covered with blue bruises. *Must be needle marks from the hospital. That's good, too.*

Margaret took another sip of tea. "I want to be compensated," she said, her face transforming into a pout, and her eyes squinting, as if focusing on some distant object. She touched her right temple. "I feel dizzy." The words were slurred and feeble; the drug had now taken effect.

"Rest your head back."

She closed her eyes and relaxed into her chair. Rupert coughed and held his chest, trying to control his pounding heart. He leaned closer to her face, watching her eyes oscillate under the lids. Then her breathing deepened, slowed, and became irregular—a clutter of sighs and guttural sounds. Her lower lip drooped, and a pool of thick saliva smeared the front of her robe. Her mouth smelled of stale tobacco.

Rupert opened his valise and removed a bottle and syringe. After filling the syringe, he found a vein in her already-bruised arm, then injected. He removed the needle and applied gentle pressure to prevent bleeding.

In her kitchen, he put on latex gloves he'd brought with him, washed the cups and saucers, and placed them in the cupboard. To moisten his mouth and ease his tongue, he drank several large glasses of cold water.

Before leaving, Rupert stood over her and smiled. He removed another vial from his valise and poured a small mound of white crystals into his palm. With deliberate care, he sparingly spread the crystals over her lying form. He closed his eyes as the Voice whispered from Judges 9:45: *Abimelech fought against the city and he took the city and he slew the people and sowed it with salt.*

Rupert stepped into the drizzle of the cool summer night. Tiny sparkles reflected from puddles on the uneven sidewalk, and the sharp scent of ozone remained strong from the recent lightning. He drew a deep breath through his nostrils and exhaled. His heart had slowed and his anger had eased. He took another refreshing breath, knowing that if he hurried, he could drop his valise at the hospital and just make the 9 p.m. feature at the Quad.

1

He said, "Bring me a new jar, and put salt in it." He went out to the spring of water, and threw salt in it and said, "Thus says the Lord, 'I have purified these waters; there shall not be from there death or unfaithfulness any longer.'"

– 2 KINGS 2:20-21

DR. MALCOLM CHRISTIAN was not offended when she said the word *mulatto*. Despite his dislike for the term and its awful history—originally referring to the offspring of a horse and a donkey, but more commonly denoting the mixture of Blackness with something else—her gentle voice made the word sound exotic, almost endearing.

Alice Wagner, a once-famous portrait artist, now eighty-five years old and dying, looked up from her sketchpad, smiling at Christian. "And your salt-and-pepper hair, Doctor, is such a nice contrast to your dark eyes. Your mother must have been very pretty."

"She was, Mrs. Wagner, and thank you," Christian said, examining the sketch she'd presented him. "I see you're still quite the artist."

He looked at the drawing. It was a skillful and flattering likeness: she'd drawn him leaning forward at her bedside, and the smile she'd given him was open and kind. The chin and jaw were strong, and the salt-and-pepper shading of his hair matched his mustache. The eyes were intelligent, penetrating, and made even more dignified by the way she fashioned the thin eyeglass frames. She captured the inch-long scar on his left cheek and shaded in his skin that left no doubt as to his mixed ethnic background. He thanked her again.

Alice smiled, happy to have pleased him. The yellow tinge to the whites of her eyes signaled that her liver was now failing along with her kidneys. She'd been diagnosed with terminal cancer, and her kidneys, invaded by the malignancy, no longer functioned. Currently, she was receiving supportive dialysis. Christian had arranged hospice for her final days, and they had agreed that her dialysis treatments would cease when she left the hospital. She would die within a month.

"I'll be back after I see the X-rays we took this morning."

"Thank you, Doctor. I'll be right here."

Minutes later, Dr. Christian walked through the door of the hospital's dialysis unit and felt the subtle change: the air, cool and sharp with disinfectant and the low background hum of the old generator, intimidating to patients and visitors alike, that should have been fixed years ago. And the other constant distractions, the annoying and discordant noises—fugue-like—from respirators and digital pumps that fed drugs and oxygen to the desperately ill. But even with these shortcomings, Christian knew the magic of this place was in the alchemy of the dialysis machines: the elegant, man-made substitute for the human kidney that purified blood and made death wait its turn.

The unit was a large rectangular area with ten treatment stations, each containing a bed, a dialysis machine, a chair, and a television set. A large nursing station occupied the center of the unit with a camera bank that monitored each station.

It was July 1, the beginning of the academic year, and Christian felt that anxiety that came with the arrival of new students, interns, and residents. As chief of the section of kidney diseases and director of dialysis, he personally supervised the teaching service every July and August. But this year, that long-established ritual would be difficult because August 31 also marked the submission deadline for the final chapters of his book.

His book, *A Grain of Salt*, would celebrate the substance that intrigued man through all ages and across all cultures. Essential to human health, it had weaved its way into man's psyche and profoundly influenced *all* aspects of his life. It was salt's miraculous immunity to decay that fascinated humans. Because of this otherworldly property, it was imbued with deep mystical and religious significance and afforded special symbolic power.

This substance had captivated Christian also, and his book would reveal how the magical combination of chlorine—a deadly gas—and sodium—a treacherous metal—had acquired such importance, unrelated to its health needs, like no other substance had, except, perhaps, gold.

Christian stopped at the nursing station and spoke to the head nurse, Crystal, a beautiful dark Haitian woman with smooth skin, hooped earrings, and two large natural braids. She motioned in the direction of his team, a hint of disappointment in her face. She showed him a clipboard. A frown tightened his expression. On the overhead speakers, Mozart's "Eine Kleine Nachtmusik" provided a bit of a light reprieve to the otherwise serious atmosphere. Together, they entered the treatment area.

Christian passed the first station, where two interns listened intently to their attending physician. They were dressed in blue isolation gowns. Their patient was attached to a respirator while simultaneously receiving dialysis. At the side of the bed, a rectal tube drained watery brown excreta into a plastic bag. A nurse, also in blue and wearing a facemask, suctioned blood-tinged mucous from the patient's nose.

At the next station, an old man, grief-stricken, watched as a woman began her treatment. A nurse adjusted the settings on the dialysis machine, directing the blood flow to and from the patient. The right thigh of the patient ended in a heavily bandaged stump, a small pink spot peeking through the white gauze. A second nurse moved swiftly about the patient, hanging a unit of blood.

A distance from the bed, a senior resident, easily distinguished by his well-fitted lab coat and muted arrogance, explained the dynamics of the dialysis procedure to a group of nursing students. A young priest, standing at the foot of the bed, placed an arm around the stooped shoulder of the old man next to him.

Christian, accompanied by Crystal, met his team at the far end of the treatment area and nodded a dignified greeting to the group. Their body language, in unison, communicated respect for his presence. He pointed a finger to one of the medical students and looked at the patient in the bed.

"Clare, bring us up to date."

"Mr. Franks is a twenty-year-old White male with a history of chronic drug addiction. He was found yesterday, semi-conscious, presumably from an overdose. He was covered with feces, and his right ankle was severely infected. His diagnoses include severe infection, massive fluid loss from diarrhea, and kidney failure. Urine and other waste products were accumulating in his blood, so emergency dialysis was started."

"What's his status now?" Christian directed this question to Dr. Kemp, the resident responsible for the immediate care of the patient.

"His foot is dead, and he'll lose the ankle. He's headed for the OR right after we're done, but low blood pressure is our problem now. He's not responding to fluids or meds."

Kemp, in his third year of training, was short and thick, with day-old stubble. His black hair was slicked back, and a thin layer of perspiration dotted his brow. His white laboratory coat was too tight and soiled. He wore no tie.

Christian, as always, began with an opening question that would lead to a teaching principle. "Why is the blood pressure not responding?" He pointed again to Clare.

"Because of the ankle infection." Her voice was crisp and self-assured.

"That's too obvious," said Christian, waving his hand aside and shaking his head. "Please be more specific."

Clare was slim with dark hair and wore bright-red lipstick. Her tight-fitting sweater and low-hugging slacks, visible under her white coat, failed to overlap at her waist.

"During serious infections, bacteria release poisons that lower the blood pressure," she responded, flipping her short bob and folding her hands in front of her.

"Correct. Can you think of any other reasons to explain the low blood pressure?"

"Salt loss," said Richard, the other medical student—tall and thin with light eyes, blond hair, and a slight stoop.

A tingle of excitement bristled the hairs on Christian's neck. "Did you say salt loss? Is there evidence for salt loss?"

"Diarrhea contains large amounts of body salt," said Richard, squinting his eyes with his precise statement.

"Does loss of body salt affect the blood pressure?" He challenged Richard.

"Salt makes up much of our blood volume. When salt is lost, the blood volume is decreased, and blood pressure falls unless the salt is replaced."

"Excellent," said Christian, clasping his hands together. "Let's see our patient."

Crystal, taking notes, nodded her approval.

The sun in the closed area intensified the stench of the decaying ankle, causing the medical students to narrow their eyes. Christian, now gloved, lifted the sheet. The lower part of the leg was packed in ice. Dark purple streaks extended up the leg. Small bubbles, filled with gas and yellow fluid, covered the gangrenous skin. Christian examined the patient's blood pressure, heart, and lungs. When he checked the intravenous fluids, his expression darkened. He shook his head and faced the group.

"The IV fluids contain only dextrose." The periodic sighs of the respirator and unremitting swish of the dialysis motor filled the silence of their space. Christian looked from face to face in the group, stopping at Dr. Kemp.

"After what's been said about salt loss and blood pressure, why isn't there any salt in the patient's replacement fluids?"

The sound of Crystal writing on the clipboard echoed in the small space. All were likely wondering whether she was taking evaluation notes.

Dr. Kemp clenched his teeth. He had made an error—a big one.

Christian carefully adjusted the knot of his blue silk tie, a perfect match to his light-blue shirt, then fastened the top button of his immaculate white lab coat. He waited a few beats, then continued. "Change all fluids to normal saline." Christian tented his fingers as if to pray. He took a deep breath and exhaled slowly in an attempt to mute his frustration.

"Remember: salt is absolutely necessary for life. Excessive loss means death." He paused. "And, inversely, too much of it will kill you. To master medicine, you must be able to manipulate this substance." He tilted his head toward Kemp, then smiled. "This relationship between salt and the blood pressure is nothing new. Four thousand years ago, Asian physicians discovered when too much salt is used in cooking, the pulse and the blood pressure, gets too high."

Christian gave Kemp a friendly and reassuring pat on the back.

"Nice shirt and tie," Crystal said as they strolled back to the nursing station at the end of rounds.

"Thank you."

"You were pretty easy on Kemp," she said, smiling. "Some of your colleagues would have made him feel like shit." Her hand brushed against his outer thigh as they were walking, and he smiled and gave her a side glance, hoping no one had seen the contact.

"He already felt like shit. No need to humiliate him any further. It's early in the month. I'll speak to him later about the mistake—and his attire—in private."

"That's why I like you. Will I see you later?"

"Where?"

"My place; I'll be alone for the weekend."

"Good."

They both stopped at the nurse's station where Christian signed several forms, then headed for his office.

Christian glanced at the picture of Dr. William Forsyth, on the wall opposite his desk. Forsyth was his first chief of medicine and mentor, and the man who had brought him to Mercy Hospital.

Twenty-five years ago, in 1966, Mercy was the leading teaching hospital in Catholic medical education in New York City. So traditional was the institution that, although more than half of its patients were Black and Hispanic, few, unless Irish or Italian, let alone a person of color, could enter the training program or gain appointment to the teaching staff. But for Christian it was different: he was in the right place, at the right time, with the right people.

Forsyth, a thin Irishman with a steel gaze and soft voice, was named Chair of Medicine the year before Christian applied for training. By that time, Forsyth had already decided to change the training program and break the unspoken policy of refusing to train minority physicians.

Christian still remembered their first meeting during his interview for the internship. Six physicians and three nuns sat at a great table, all of them with chalk-white faces and red cheeks. The nuns had empathetic smiles; the physicians all wore curious and appraising looks, their awkwardness apparent because few Black candidates had ever gotten this far in the application process. Forsyth sat at the head of the table, and he, alone, asked questions.

At the end of the session, Dr. Forsyth followed him into the hallway. He placed a hand on Christian's shoulder and said, "I want you to train at Mercy." He squeezed Christian's shoulder as he spoke. "I want you to train here in medicine because I think you'd be the right person. Can you give me your word?"

An intern position at Mercy Hospital was a coveted prize in New York City. But the matching system strictly prohibited making any binding agreements during interviews. An official matching procedure was to be followed. For a moment, Christian wondered whether Forsyth was testing his integrity. He'd looked into the face of many White men—men with power over his life; many were dismissive, others condescending, and some outright bigots. But the look in Forsyth's eyes was different. Christian answered, "Yes." So in 1967 Malcolm Christian began his internship at Mercy Hospital.

Christian finished the rigorous first year and was awarded Intern of the Year. He knew he'd been a good intern but wasn't convinced he'd deserved that honor. He never wanted special treatment, but he realized that this Irishman was a friend and was giving him a push.

Under Forsyth's mentoring and general teaching philosophy, Christian thrived. He was treated with the same respect and deference as all the other trainees. Christian advanced through the medical residency and the fellowship in kidney diseases with splendid performances, graduating from the program with the most coveted prize: the William Osler Medal.

Christian spent the next two years directing the busy kidney division at the US Naval Hospital in Boston. Despite the heavy demands of patient care and training interns and residents, Christian wrote a landmark paper on the effects of severe burns and combat injuries on kidney function. Before his discharge from the navy, he was invited to join the faculty of several prestigious New York hospitals, but he chose to return to Mercy. This was his home, and Forsyth was his chief.

Christian accepted the position of associate chief of the section of nephrology, and, within three years, his reputation as a teacher and his popularity with the private practitioners, led to his appointment as chief. Now, in 1992, besides being professor of medicine and head of his section, he served as chairman of the committee on academics and credentials. After twenty-five years, his bibliography consisted of sixteen peer-reviewed papers and national recognition as a teacher, clinician, and researcher.

Christian studied the face of Dr. Forsyth and reflected on what this man had done for him long before affirmative action was popular. Forsyth was a kind and just man. He believed in the Golden Rule, and he preached that mentoring was as important as teaching facts. He was a gentleman and would never embarrass a trainee in front of a group; yet he would never tolerate anyone presenting for rounds wearing soiled whites. He would say: "Clean hands, clipped nails, and well-groomed. Begin each day immaculate."

Christian would meet with Kemp and review the need for salt replacement in this case, and he would also discuss the need for proper attire on rounds. With each topic he would be a mentor following in the footsteps of the man who gave him his break in life.

2

Why does salt when thrown into fire crackle? Is it because salt contains a little moisture, which is converted into vapor by the heat and driven apart by force, separates the salt? However, does everything that is separated crackle?

- ARISTOTLE, *NAT. HIST.*, XXXI, 85

HOMICIDE DETECTIVE ALEX LUGANOS turned his chair to face the two noisy detectives across the room. "Valdez! Rashid! Keep it down!"

He shook his head and closed his worn copy of *The Iliad*, placing it next to the neat stack of files on his desk. The dull pain in his stomach was just starting, and he was glad he'd taken his acid-killing pill an hour earlier.

He looked at the picture of his father on the wall next to his desk. They were holding hands, and Luganos, still just a boy, held the Greek flag. His father, medium height, broad shoulders, dark eyes and hair, and characteristic patrician bearing, was smiling. This was his mother's favorite picture. "You looked like twins," she used to say.

Luganos, now fifty—the age his father was when the picture was taken—saw the strong resemblance, but noted his own older-looking reflection in the glass. Smoking and chronic acne had aged his face; nonetheless, his dark eyes, dark hair, and Grecian nose were enough to make him handsome, like his father.

The night that picture was taken, his father told him, "Kalymnos, my birthplace, sent two ships to fight at Troy under the leadership of Agamemnon. Our family's blood can be traced all the way back to the Trojan War. Be proud you are Greek. You must, because even in this great city, Greeks never get anywhere. Now, it's the Blacks, Latinos, and Russian Jews in Brooklyn who get the breaks."

Luganos looked back at Rashid, with his two pierced ears and mismatched earrings, and at Valdez, who had a shaved head, a meticulously styled beard, and pointed sideburns. *These jokers will make detective in less than five,* he thought to himself.

His phone rang, and he picked up: "Detective Luganos."

"I'm gonna be late; got a 1069." It was Precinct Detective Ralph Duggan, frustration evident in his voice.

"How long?"

"Don't know. Old lady, dead a few days."

"What time does the Knicks game start?"

"Seven-thirty. Come on the call, maybe save some time?"

"Meet you out front."

Luganos slowly shook his head as he hung up the phone. "That's Duggan. He's going to be fuckingggg late."

"Shit, man, not again," said Valdez.

"I'm tagging along to speed things up."

As a rule, homicide detectives didn't see cases unless there was a definite homicide or a high suspicion of one. The precinct detective saw all other deaths initially. As Luganos put on his jacket to leave, he reminded himself that he was only a bystander and would keep his mouth shut.

Duggan and Luganos arrived at Twenty-Second Street and Third Avenue, a nice block, but noisy. Outside the dead woman's apartment, Duggan greeted Patrolman Ryan with a handshake; Luganos gave a slight nod of his head.

"You first on the scene?" Duggan asked.

"Yeah, the building's superintendent called because of the smell from the apartment and nobody was answering the door. Found her when we got in. Doors and windows locked."

Ryan was tall, wiry, and Black. Both of his muscular arms were covered with tattoos.

"Who noticed the smell?"

"Lady next door. Said she hadn't heard the woman in a couple of days." Ryan pointed across the hall to the only other apartment on the floor. The door opened, and a short elderly lady, a handkerchief covering her nose, stepped into the hall.

"I'm Mrs. Stanley, gentlemen," the woman called out. "She came out of the hospital about a week ago."

"I'm Detective Duggan, and this is Detective Luganos. When's the last time you spoke to her?"

"Oh, we never speak, but I hear her every day and always smell her cigarettes in the hallway." The old lady leaned her head to one side, attempting to hide a slight tremor. "It's been so quiet—and that awful smell! I knew something was wrong."

"Did you notice anything else?" Duggan asked.

"No."

"Thank you, Mrs. Stanley. We may need to speak to you again."

The woman, bright-eyed behind the handkerchief, slowly backed into her apartment and closed the door. Covering their noses, the three men entered the dead woman's apartment.

Duggan immediately coughed. "Shit, at *least* three days."

Luganos saw the body on the couch. The greenish skin of the face was starting to detach from the muscle layers below. Dark fluid seeped from the open mouth and nostrils, and a damp, discolored pillow lay beneath the lower half of the woman's body. The smell was overwhelming.

"Definitely more than three days," said Luganos, tightening his jaw as he swallowed.

Duggan leaned close, inspecting the seepage from the nose and mouth. "No maggots?"

"The windows were closed," replied Luganos. "No flies could get in." *He should know that.* Recently, he'd noticed Duggan's red complexion, weight gain, and heavy breathing. There was talk that he was drinking on the job again.

"Are those her medications?" Duggan pointed to the prescription bottles on a desk against the wall. Ryan stood by the open window taking a deep breath of air, sunlight playing off a tattooed heart on his neck.

"Yeah," said Ryan. "The superintendent used to pick them up for her."

"Who opened the window?"

"I did," said Ryan, mild defensiveness in his voice.

"Were you gloved?"

"Of course."

"The rest of the place?"

"Clean." Ryan exhaled heavily.

Duggan opened a drawer and looked through the contents. "This must be her doctor," he said, holding up a sheet of paper. Luganos signaled he was going into the bedroom. Duggan dialed the doctor's number on his cell phone.

When Luganos returned to the living room, Duggan had finished his call.

"She had a bad ticker. No family and just got out of the hospital. Doctor said she was smoking herself to death."

Luganos stood over the deceased, fingering an inflamed pimple on his rough chin. He bent on one knee, lowering his eyes to the level of the table in front of the couch. "What's this stuff?"

"Huh?" Duggan looked at the white crystals scattered on the clean table, then looked at his watch. He walked off toward the kitchen.

Luganos, still kneeling, removed the glove from his left hand, moistened the tip of his index finger, and tasted several crystals. He frowned. Luganos then followed Duggan into the small kitchen. They inspected the sink, refrigerator, and several cabinets.

Returning to where the dead woman lay, Duggan rubbed his palms together and pointed to Ryan. "What do you think?"

"No signs of violence, door and windows locked, all those medications. Looks like it could be her heart."

Duggan nodded in agreement. "I'll call the medical examiner, and they can take the body." He took out his new Dycam 1 digital camera and photographed the scene from multiple angles.

Duggan walked into the fading sunlight whistling. Luganos followed right behind, not whistling. Instead, he pondered several thoughts. First, he was pleased they'd get to the game on time but peeved that Ryan didn't know that "yeah" was a disrespectful answer to a question from a superior. The other item, though subtle, was bothersome: he didn't see any salt or saltshaker in the kitchen. He tucked this away for later consideration. As they pulled away from the curb, Duggan lit a cigarette, took a deep drag, then coughed. Luganos opened the window and took a breath. The slight discomfort in his stomach had eased, and the hint of salt so strong on his taste buds minutes ago, was slowly fading away.

3

The wise man puts a pinch of sugar in everything he says to the other and listens with a grain of salt to what the other says.

– PLINY THE ELDER

"WE ARE IN DEEP SHIT," Greenberg said, looking up from his cluttered desk.

"What are you talking about?" asked Christian.

"We're dead broke. We got no money. The bishops spent all our money on two bullshit institutions."

Alf Greenberg was the director of medicine at Mercy Hospital. An oily sheen covered his brow, and a full blond unkempt beard covered his distinctly Nordic-looking face. Sweat dampened his shirt collar, and his light intelligent eyes were red from strain.

Years ago, Greenberg was a year behind Christian at Mercy. They were a special duo—a Jew and a Negro—facing the hardships of training in the most conservative Catholic-Irish-Italian-dominated hospital in New York City.

"So, what happens now?" asked Christian.

Greenberg held up a sheet of paper. "We need fifty million, and the archdioceses' got the cash. But we're not the only show in town. St. Mary's is ready to tank, and that's a problem. The lawyers are looking at her financials as we speak. Father Joseph—that pious sneak—is doing the audits, and he'll make the final decision. If you remember, I wasn't exactly his choice for this job. He wanted a Catholic—that guy from Georgetown. And that's why you're here."

"That's why I'm here? What does that mean?" Christian leaned forward in his chair.

"You're the only Catholic section chief in this hospital. All the rest are Jews, Arabs or Indians or whatever. Plus, you're Black."

"Okay, I'm Black. Did you just discover that?"

"I'm talking about politics and practicality. Times have changed. He's got to be civil to you—*politically correct*, if you get my drift."

"Who?"

"Father Joseph."

"Hey—you think he's going to give us money because I'm Black?"

"No, but he'll be polite and listen to whatever you have to say. He's got to." Greenberg got up from his desk. "That's the trend, now. Besides, you know this place; you've served on all the committees, the residents love you, and you've done good research." Greenberg walked over to the window and looked out. "He's not gonna give me the fucking time of day, but he's got to treat you civil."

Greenberg walked back to his desk, picked up a folder, then slammed it down. "I'm assigning you as his point man—the go-to-guy for general bullshit: the academic program, the committee stuff, and credentialing. You won't have to do much; he'll be spending his time with the bookkeepers, and thank God, they're all Catholic. He'll want some kind of written report, which I'll do. I'm putting you at his disposal twenty-four seven."

"This is bullshit." Christian sat back in defiance.

"Yeah, but you're still the only Catholic section chief, and you're still Black—fair-skinned, nonetheless—but Black. Look, I need you. Since

I've been chief, I've given you everything you asked for—and I mean *everything*! A fucking raise, two new computers, and that silly-ass microwave oven for the residents' work room."

The wall behind Greenberg's desk was filled with awards and photographs tastefully arranged and in marked contrast to his messy desk. Two photos showed Greenberg and Christian receiving awards during their training.

"We're better than St. Mary's, but *all* their section chiefs are Catholic and that fucking counts! Most of this shit is political, and you know it! We gotta get his ear. I can't trust this to anyone else. We're setting up an office for him and giving him a secretary. He'll be here in three days to check things out."

Greenberg narrowed his eyes at Christian. "Didn't you go to Catholic school?"

"For six months when I was ten. Then I moved."

"That's good enough."

"Alf, I'm not a practicing Catholic. I don't go to church; I don't even remember my prayers. I've heard this guy is old-school."

"Then go to church while he's here. Let him see you in the chapel praying and taking Communion. There's a mass every morning at seven a.m. for the faithful. The name of the game is bullshit and money! This guy is business, doesn't like things out of place. No drama, no fuss, no publicity, and everything low key."

"Alf, I'm on the teaching service for the next two months. It's July and you know what that means. Besides, all my people have their assignments. They can't spell me; I can't ask them to change now. Plus, I've got my book to complete. I'm overloaded."

"If we don't get that money, *everyone* will be looking for a job, including you. You gotta step up and help me. I need you to do this." A lock of unruly hair fell across Greenberg's eyes, despite his efforts to brush it aside.

"What happens if he *isn't* politically correct?"

"You'll be looking for a job with the rest of us."

Greenberg opened the thick folder on his desk, signaling that the conversation was over.

"You need a haircut," Christian said as he got up to leave.

Upset, Christian took the stairs instead of the elevator to think things through. *Twenty-five years ago, I was lucky to get my foot in the front door of this place, and now he's using me because I'm Black. This is bullshit.*

Christian didn't like being on display. The same thing happened when he was the only Black doctor on staff at the Naval Hospital. During the yearly inspections from Washington, he was deliberately invited—no, paraded—at every function. *Funny, today, twice being reminded that he was different on the whims of political correctness.*

It was one thing to help Greenberg with the priest, but, sadly, Christian knew he was not chosen because he was highly respected as a physician and teacher, or even because he was the credentialing officer of the institution. It was his social identity—his race—that made him valuable, now. It was insulting. But what could he do? How could he say no?

It was true that Greenberg had given him everything he'd asked for. He owed Greenberg, but more than that, he owed Forsyth. Mercy had been Forsyth's whole life, and Christian felt obligated.

Greenberg and he had been close, but Christian had misgivings about his friend. During his training, Greenberg quickly brown-nosed the senior residents and became their pet. He never took off a Jewish holiday, and that got him big points. Besides being articulate and an excellent physician, Greenberg was a master politician. Now, he was scheming to put Father Joseph in a difficult spot. To make the situation worse, Greenberg would let it be known that Christian was playing a major role in the audit, and, if things went wrong, then obviously Christian had been ineffective and partially to blame.

When Christian got back to his office, he looked at his manuscript and pondered the four chapters he'd yet to complete. It had taken him five years to write *A Grain of Salt*, and he'd made up his mind that nothing would prevent him from completing the manuscript on time.

He would do as requested, but not at the expense of the book. He'd use Greenberg's plan to his own advantage. Until the audit was complete, he would ask Dr. Barvey, his associate chief, to cover the dialysis unit, and residents' needs, and request Dr. Rohmart, his new young attending, to cover morning rounds, leaving only one morning and afternoon clinic and his private patients for him to cover himself. He would have time to meet with the priest, but more importantly, he'd steal the time to work on his book.

This was the first time Christian chose to put his wishes before anything else. He'd always done more than was required, validating himself as the dependable Black guy doing more than expected. That was his life to this point; that's how he'd been trained to think and function.

"You have to be twice as good and make no waves—you know that," his stepfather used to say.

Well, not this time. Yes, he loved teaching, mentoring, caring for patients, and the spotlight of the podium, but now he wanted something more: to produce something original—literary. He took a deep breath, promising that he'd do all he could to save Forsyth's hospital, but the book came first.

Christian took two Tylenols and left his office, his manuscript under his arm.

4

*For its taste and for its harmonious strength,
salt has become a divine substance, most
beloved to the Gods.*

~ PLATO

CRYSTAL ANSWERED THE DOOR in her bathrobe. She was wearing a string of pearls. She'd taken a shower, and her braids were wrapped in a white towel, accentuating her coco-brown complexion.

The foyer of her apartment was small, and when they brushed against each other, she smiled, acknowledging his obvious arousal. The cramped space amplified the sweet aroma of her skin and her coconut-scented shampoo. He could smell the faint balmy wetness of her own excitement.

"I thought you might not come," she said.

"I almost didn't."

"Why?" She pulled out of their embrace and tilted her head back to look at him, her smile measured yet seductive. Her body pushed softly against his excitement.

"We need money, or they're going to close us down."

"I know."

"You know? How?"

"Never you mind." She handed him a glass. "There's your drink; I made it myself from a recipe in a book." Crystal's robe fell open as she handed him the drink.

She took his jacket and laid it next to her nursing uniform.

"That's good," Christian said, pointing to the margarita after taking a sip.

She looked at him whimsically. "You do know the hospital's policy on fraternization between staff, especially since I directly report to you?"

"I do."

They'd slept together twice several weeks ago at a conference in Washington, DC. On each occasion, nothing had been planned. It had just happened, and they'd both enjoyed it.

They sat next to each other on the couch. Her arm was around his shoulder, and his hand rested on her bare thigh. In her living room, two large framed watercolor scenes of Haiti and several black-and-white photos were tastefully displayed.

He kissed her forehead, then her cheek. She exhaled, a warm breath, flavored by the fruity bite of the tequila, as his hands cupped her breasts and gently caressed her nipples. They kissed, and he passed his tongue lightly over her lips, moving his head from side to side.

She guided him into her darkened bedroom, where he removed her robe, then undressed. She slipped into bed, and he followed. He kissed her breast and licked her belly. His hand gently moved between her legs. As he started to enter her, he felt another pair of hands on his back and another set of lips on his neck.

He looked to the side, startled, suddenly aware of a different perfume—aromatic, like licorice, maybe anise?—as the stranger's voice playfully whispered, "Party time."

Before he left, they stood together in the small foyer.

"I knew you would like it, but I didn't think it would be your first time," Crystal said, smiling.

"It was my first time, and I very much liked it. It was quite exciting." Christian felt groggy, both from the tequila and from the events in bed.

"No introductions, just surprise. My friend likes it that way. So far, it's only been with girls. Good night, Professor."

"Good night, Crystal."

5

*There is nothing can be brought forth in the
nature of things, without the medium of salt . . .
The sun and salt are the parents of all things.*

– JOHANN RUDOLPH GLAUBER

RUPERT FELT THE DEEP SORENESS in the fold of his left arm. He passed his fingers over the hardened veins, now useless and destroyed by the countless times they were punctured to save his life. He strained to make a fist in his left hand and failed. He flexed both wrists, and the bones ached. He rested back in bed, hoping the feeling in his arm would soon return and listened as the Voice, quiet so far today, quoted Ezekiel 16:4: *And as for thy nativity in the day thou wast born, thy navel was not cut, neither was thou washed in water to smooth thee, not salted at all.*

He licked his parched lips and took his pulse, then walked to the bathroom. With effort, he released a burning stream of urine, his face contorting as he held the wall for support. Rupert then reached for the aromatic cologne and massaged it into his hands and face. Avoiding the mirror as he left the bathroom, he inhaled and slowly smiled; the fragrance of the cologne was just enough to satisfy his fantasy of being normal.

Tell me your story again, please! asked the Voice as he climbed back into bed. Kneading the aching arm, legs stretched out, he rested back on the pillow.

Please? the Voice asked again.

A pause, then Rupert began: "My mother said that Lisa, the nurse in the baby unit, told her, 'Your boy is tiny, and his skin is pale. His cry is weak and his blood pressure keeps falling. The doctors are worried.'

"Suspecting impending shock from internal bleeding, Lisa removed my diaper to check for blood. She saw the cluster of white crystals at the end of my penis. When the doctors came, they said the salt in my blood was low—very low—dripping out of my body through my kidneys. The white stuff at the end of my penis was salt crystals. They called me a 'salt loser'—a mistake of nature—something like a freak, leaking my life away in my pee. They said I would be dead by morning."

A door slammed in the next apartment, causing Rupert to jump and released a deep moan. With his eyes filled with tears, he turned his body to the wall and drifted to sleep as the Voice sang "Amazing Grace" a cappella, in the fashion a British choirboy.

6

*Salt is pure, white, immaculate, an incorruptible
a substance . . . indispensable to human beings.
It has correspondingly been regarded as the
essence of things in general; the quintessence
of life, and the very soul of the body . . .
and its immunity against decay made
it an emblem of immortality.*

~ ERNEST JONES

DR. CHRISTIAN TOOK A SIP OF WATER and looked into his audience. This was the first year he'd been invited to participate in the Dean's Lecture Series for the Public at The New School. He loved being at the podium, in the spotlight of the dark auditorium. He would begin by discussing "Salt in Health and Disease," then expand on the theme, "Salt: Mysterious and Everywhere."

"Man has a craving for salt and seeks it to stay alive. It's a physiologic necessity; a desperate appetite that must be satisfied, even if it means drinking the blood of an enemy he's just slaughtered." An elderly, white-haired lady in the front row grimaced and looked into her lap.

Christian paused and took a long stare at his audience. "There's much more to the story of salt; Homer, for example, referred to it as a divine substance, and Plato said it was a food dear to the Gods." Christian noted that these references to salt occurred four thousand years before Christ and explained that the Bible, with its thirty-two salt citations, was called the first book of salt. "And, so precious was this substance in parts of the world," Christian continued, "that it became the favored substitute for money. Roman soldiers were paid part of their earnings in salt; hence the word, 'salary' and the phrase, 'A soldier worth his salt.'

"It wasn't long after discovering salt's ability to prevent decay, especially of meat, that man christened it *sacred*. It was due to this *preservative power*—this miraculous gift—that salt became imbued with deep mystical and religious significance; so much so that it became emblematic of durability and permanence. And any agreement made under the blessing of salt could never be broken."

Christian paused, his left hand resting on the podium; smiled; then raised his right hand and shook his index finger in warning. "A covenant of salt cannot be broken."

"Everywhere we turn, salt is in our history. In France, for example, the *gabelle*—the hated salt tax—sparked the French Revolution, and in India, Gandhi used the British salt tax to start the Independence Movement.

"And in Norway, 'One will shed as many tears as may suffice to dissolve the quantity of salt spilled,' and folks from Yorkshire lament, 'Every grain of salt spilled represents a tear to be shed in the future.' And so meaningful was the symbolism of salt that, Jesus, on the Mount of Olives, said to the faithful, 'Ye are the salt of the earth.'

"Wherever you look, salt symbolism is found in our religious practices, our literature, our art, our blessings, and curses. Over time, however, we've forgotten how this substance has shaped our psyche and our lives."

At the end of his talk, Christian looked at his watch, then fastened the top button of his jacket. "This would be a good place to stop. I'll pick things up in my second talk." Folding his notes, he turned to Dean

Rayburn, the chairman of the night's program. Rayburn walked to the podium and placed an arm around Christian's shoulder.

Rayburn spoke in a deep, elegant voice, modulated by years of addressing cultured groups: "The bad news is we must vacate the room. The good news is we'll return in two weeks and again play host to Dr. Christian. I'm told he'll have more to say about his favorite topic and, in addition, treat us to more from his upcoming book on this fascinating subject."

The audience applauded.

∞

Christian arrived home filled with enthusiasm from the evening's lecture. Enlivened, he sat in his living room, the manuscript of his book in front of him. He no longer feared the subject would be boring to his readers. Tonight, the audience was absolutely engrossed; Christian felt he'd gotten it right.

He looked over at the gold-framed picture of his mother, perfectly centered and placed apart from the other pictures on the mantle. This was how he remembered her: her dark-brown skin, sensuous eyes, and full lips. Her hair, short and freshly straightened; her teeth, brilliant white; and her smile, as always, measured and flirtatious. She was seventeen when the picture was taken, just two years after his birth.

His mother could barely read or write, a fact unknown to him until he was in his teens and never discovered by her friends. But she was a woman full of stories: when he was seven years old, she'd held him close and said, "My sister, Dotty, delivered you exactly at the stroke of midnight. She placed cobwebs on your navel to protect you from evil spirits, and the next day, she prepared special biscuits of flour and salt to please all the spirits because your afterbirth was dark. Dotty said you would sleep with a light on and one day write a book about magic."

He knew his mother believed in night ghosts, in omens and the sly Devil. Once, she'd told him she'd seen a ghost. This frightened him, but most of the time, she said she saw kind angels. When she left him in the mornings at the babysitter's house, after they had come to new York, he would sit in the dimly lit living room while the babysitter's family slept, wondering if the strange sounds he heard were those of a ghost walking about.

He thought back to a time in Harlem when it was just the two of them, so long ago he'd forgotten the year. They lived on the first floor of a small brownstone with a large window that overlooked the street. It was a hot summer night and just turning dark. Suddenly, they heard loud footsteps, and someone yelled, "Help!" When they went outside, in the bright cone of a streetlight, a man lay in the gutter, moaning and bleeding from his face. The neighborhood gangs sometimes fought at night, but he'd never seen anything like this. The man in the street was White. There were no White gangs in his neighborhood.

A crowd stood watching, but no one was helping the man. Christian, then too young to know the history of resentment, quickly understood from the whispers that the man was not to be helped. This was a White man. Christian heard someone in the crowd say the night before, three White policemen beat a Black teenager to death. Someone else yelled, "They killed that boy last night because he was Black." Christian was confused: he was taught that policemen were good; and he wondered what the boy had done wrong. He couldn't believe that a boy could be killed because of his color.

Without saying a word, his mother took Christian back to their apartment. There, she filled a basin of water and gathered a pillow and several clean towels. Before leaving the apartment, she placed her hands on his shoulders and looked into his eyes. "Be brave."

His mother slowly walked back and pushed her way through the muttering crowd. She knelt beside the man and gently placed his head on the pillow and washed the blood from his face. Christian would never forget how fast his heart was beating as he sat beside her. There were threats from the crowd, and he feared something would happen to his mother when all of this was over.

Soon the police came. Then an ambulance arrived. He held his mother's hand, and she stayed with the man until they took him away.

That night, as they sat on his bed, aware of this new closeness between them, he asked his mother if she'd been frightened when she helped the man.

"Yes, very frightened," she told him.

"Why did you help him when no one else did?"

His mother held both his hands and said: "You must always do the right thing, even if it means going against your friends, or, like tonight, those angry people. One day you will come to know why the people were angry. They have good cause to be mad, but that doesn't mean *you* should turn away from doing what is right. We did good, you did good; it was the right thing to do." She pulled him close. "Tonight, you were the perfect son, a little warrior. It didn't surprise me; I know you have a warrior's blood in your veins. One day I'll tell you that story."

The next morning his mother told him that the man had died.

Christian looked from her face to the three maps of Africa elegantly displayed on the wall above the burgundy sofa. One of them depicted the Bight of Benin—a center of the slave trade. He then looked at the framed close-up photographs of the solemn faces of Bud Powell and an overweight Charlie Parker. His eyes move to an adjacent wall to a framed napkin autographed by John Coltrane, and next to it, two sepia pictures one of Sitting Bull and a full standing shot of Emiliano Zapata. He smiled at a framed letter he'd received from Bertrand Russell.

He turned and looked Behind his writing desk to the seven freehand drawings: two of Bach and one each of Beethoven, Shakespeare, Martin Luther King, Malcolm X, and the haunting face of the self-taught Hindi mathematical genius, Ramanujan.

On a separate wall, illuminated by a lamp, his eyes settled on the classic reprint of a slave ship and its Black cargo, bound in chains, and meticulously arranged in tight rows—head to feet—destined for the land of the free.

Christian was born in Nassau, the Bahamas, in a poor section called "Over-the-Hill." He was born out of wedlock; no birth certificate was issued. According to his mother, a cripple priest came and baptized him and later entered into the parish records the birth of one mulatto male born at midnight in Over-the-Hill.

Christian took a shower and went to bed with the light on in his bedroom.

7

*The corrupt worm corrupts all things,
and there is nothing on earth, neither woods
nor foods nor earth nor flesh, which it does
not consume save salt and oil.*

– EUTHYMIOS

RUPERT SMILED AT THE HUGE MAN sitting before him and replayed their conversation from four nights before. Rocco had come to St. Mary's Emergency Room with an infected toe and dangerously high blood sugar. The ER doctor recommended immediate admission for treatment. Rocco became foul-mouthed and disrespectful.

Shifting his gaze away from the snoring man, Rupert began to look around the room. The rug, a mixture of matted grime and bare patches, was smooth and shiny like the murky surface of the subway platform at West Fourth Street. Rupert had found the filthy place unbearable and had wanted to leave as soon as he'd arrived, but he resisted the impulse. He would complete his task and rid this man of sin.

Rupert remembered how he'd tried to reason with Rocco at the hospital: "This is serious; your toe is infected." *How could he treat his body this way?* he recalled thinking to himself.

Rocco hadn't cared. "Just give me the damn antibiotics so I can get outta here."

"That toe won't heal at home. If you leave, you must sign out against medical advice. That's hospital policy."

"I'm not signing shit." The big man farted loudly and laughed.

"That's not funny. You need to pay better attention to your hygiene."

"What's that supposed to mean?"

"Your feet are filthy, Mr. Rocco."

"Hey, Mr. Big Shot, you don't look so healthy yourself. You're pale as shit."

"Health is a special gift from God; you should respect that gift."

"Think you're a wise guy, huh? I'm gonna make a complaint. You got no right to call a patient filthy."

"As you wish, Mr. Rocco; I'll be more than happy to get you the proper forms."

Now, Rocco was asleep, put that way by a sweet drink he couldn't refuse. The Voice in Rupert's head said, *There's need for healing in this place, alive with the Devil and decay!*

The fat man's arm was thick, cold, and sweaty, making it difficult to find a vein. Rupert inserted the needle and then swore under his breath as blood escaped from the torn vessel creating a blue blot under the skin.

If you weren't so fat, I would have hit the vein perfectly.

Rupert leaned close to Rocco, applying pressure to the leaking vessel and turning his face to avoid the man's odor. Rupert tried again, and, finding a vein, injected, but not slowly. He delivered the entire contents of the syringe in one plunge, with spite.

Still sitting upright, the sleeping man's quiet breathing suddenly became irregular, and his arms and legs began to jerk, forcing his body to bolt forward, his head striking the table in front of the couch. Another wave of jerking followed, this time more violent, bending Rocco's body in half, causing him to expel a massive mixture of gas and shit as he lost consciousness.

In Rocco's bathroom the sink was filthy. The soap dish was slimy and matted with hair. A dark ring of grime encircled the face bowl. Hardened particles of food were crusted inside the bowl, and debris obstructed the drain. Rupert vomited twice, as much from his own illness as from the unsavory surroundings and the body-stink of his victim. He washed repeatedly to remove the smell of Rocco from his hands.

When Rupert spread the crystals over the dead man, the Voice recited Rupert's favorite verse from the text of Ignatius of Antioch: *Be salted in him so that no one among you may be corrupted, and by your odor . . . you will be tested!*

Before leaving the apartment, Rupert rubbed a Band-Aid over the dirty floor to give it a worn appearance and placed it over the failed attempt. He was displeased that his first needle stick was botched and worried that the blood leak under the skin might draw undue attention.

∞

As he walked in the direction of St. Mary's Hospital, where he would work that night, Rupert slipped two salt tablets into his mouth directly from the bottle and swallowed without water. Even though he'd washed thoroughly, he didn't want to touch the tablets; he could still smell Rocco's stench on his hands.

8

What a funny planet (the Earth). It is ugly, dry, and full of sharp points and is all salty.

– ANTOINE DE SAINT-EXUPÉRY

DETECTIVE LUGANOS FINISHED his second hot dog and softly massaged the center of his chest. He'd forgotten to take his pill, and the pain of reflux was just beginning.

He watched two young Black men step from a gleaming red Lexus at the corner of Sixth Avenue and Eighth Street. To Luganos, the lyrics blasting from the speakers were unintelligible, but he caught several vulgar phrases. Both men walked with a comfortable swagger, and by chance—or maybe deliberately—bumped him as they entered a Gray's Papaya hot dog restaurant. Luganos said nothing.

The taller of the two men had long dreadlocks and sported a row of gleaming gold teeth that perfectly matched his oversized earrings. He wore a black mesh tank top over an impressive physique. He caught Luganos's eye as he passed, an air of insolence in his slightly challenging gaze. The shorter of the two, also with a sculpted body, wore a black do-rag and walked with his legs spread apart to support his beltless baggy pants, which he wore so low, his yellow underwear was on display.

Luganos fingered the sore pimple on his chin and shook his head. *Be careful, Leroy,* he thought to himself. *Those sensitivity classes won't help your ass today . . .*

Luganos's cell phone rang. It was from the precinct dispatcher—a possible homicide. He drove away with mixed feelings: excited by the call but unhappy that he didn't have time for a chat with the two men regarding the noise and the shoulder bump.

∞

Luganos stopped outside the building at Third Avenue and Fourteenth Street. Unlike most of the other policewomen, Patrolwoman Novella Smith wore a subtle cologne. She greeted him with a smile as he exited the elevator.

"What have we got?"

"Sort of iffy: big guy with a bump on his head. The precinct wanted you to take a look."

In the dead man's apartment, Smith squinted from the odor but kept the handkerchief away from her nose as she spoke. "Nothing's been touched. The visiting nurse was in the apartment less than five minutes. She's downstairs in the lobby with the superintendent."

Luganos covered his own nose with a handkerchief. He saw the body bent over the coffee table, but decided to look through the apartment first, motioning Smith to follow.

In the kitchen, dirty dishes covered the sink, and the garbage can was overflowing. The tiny bathroom smelled of urine and was cluttered with adult magazines and open food containers. In the cramped bedroom, the unmade cot was covered with soiled underwear, and a large pile of dirty and foul smelling towels rested in a corner. Several pregnant roaches carrying their egg capsules and undisturbed by the visitors, crawled slowly along the walls.

"Anything else?" asked Luganos as they walked back into living room.

"The nurse said he was diabetic, and his sugar was always high. Said he'd gone to the emergency room last week with a toe infection, and she hadn't heard from him since. She visits twice a month but talks to him on the phone at least once a week."

The living room had one large upholstered chair, a gray sofa, and a chipped glass coffee table. The cushions of the sofa were covered with stains.

Rocco was bent at the waist, part of him on the couch and part of him on the coffee table. His eyes were open. A small cut surrounded by matted black blood was on the left side of his forehead. His face was mottled and gray.

Luganos pointed to the cut on Rocco's head. "Is this why they called homicide?"

"Yes."

"Anything else?"

"No." Smith moved across the room and pointed to an array of candies including several open packs of sugar-coated gummies on a small side table. "He certainly liked his sweets."

"So I've noticed," said the detective.

Luganos's eyes shifted away from Rocco's head and settled on the white substance on the coffee table. The white grains were also on Rocco's shoulders, his back, and in his hair.

Smith, standing close by, watched as Luganos removed one of his gloves, pressed a moist finger onto several crystals, and then placed his finger to the tip of his tongue.

"Sweet?" Smith asked, moving closer, a frown on her face.

"No," he said without turning from the dead man. "What do you think?"

She surveyed the scene again. "No signs of any struggle. The cut might have happened when his head hit the table. Could have been a heart attack or a stroke. That toe looks awful."

As the salty crystals dissolved in his mouth, Luganos felt his pulse increase. His heart was pumping harder. He delicately fingered the pimple on his chin, his cool exterior disguising his excitement.

"Do we call the precinct detectives back?" she asked.

"No, Officer Smith. Let's call the crime unit, instead. The head wound bothers me."

∞

Luganos waited until the crime unit completed its work and then spoke to Dr. Giles, the medical examiner.

"What do you think?" asked Luganos, offering Giles a cigarette.

Giles removed his rubber gloves and accepted the cigarette, "I doubt the head wound killed the guy."

"What do you think made his head hit the table?" Luganos pursed his lips and tilted his own head to the side.

"Can't say. It doesn't look like foul play—at least not yet. The guy was a big health risk: obese, diabetic, on blood pressure meds, and infected, from the looks of that toe."

"You'll do toxicology?"

Giles looked at his watch. "The works."

∞

The fresh air and the bright sunlight relieved the gloom of the death scene. In his car, after lighting a cigarette, Luganos sat and looked at the digital pictures he'd taken upstairs with his new camera.

After placing a call, Luganos drove downtown, wondering why Giles hadn't mentioned the crystals on Rocco's body. *Did he think they were sugar crystals from the packs of candies that Officer Smith pointed out? Or was he being cautious with his observations, like me?*

As he drove, Luganos reviewed Smith's performance. He was disappointed that she hadn't followed up when he said the crystals weren't sweet. He wondered whether Smith had a boyfriend. She didn't wear a wedding ring. He liked her smooth brown skin and dark eyes. He'd never been with a Black woman, and the thought of her skin against white sheets excited him. He wondered whether she shaved between her legs.

Luganos found two Tums in the glove compartment and placed them in his mouth. As his acid reflux eased, he narrowed his eyes, trying to figure out how the hell salt had ended up in Rocco's right car.

9

That there must be something strangely sacred in salt: it is found in our tears and in the sea.

~ GIBRAN KAHLIL GIBRAN

CHIEF WILBER R. DEWEY was a big man with red hair, large hands, and a ruddy complexion. Before joining the force, he'd spent eight years in the Marines, the last three as a drill sergeant. He grew up in Back Bay, Boston, with two sisters: one was a grade-school teacher in the Catholic school he'd once attended, and the other was a nun—a Sister of Charity—who worked in hospice.

Dewey glanced up from his desk as Luganos walked into his office.

"You look concerned, Alex," Dewey observed, closing a folder.

"Possibly."

"What's up?"

"Ten days ago, I tagged along with Duggan on a 1069. The case looked routine, natural causes, probable heart attack."

"You said *looked* routine. It wasn't?"

Luganos stopped at the interruption, shifted in his chair, then began again: "There were white crystals scattered on the deceased and on a nearby table."

"Crystals? What kind?"

"White crystals—like sugar or salt."

"So?"

Luganos picked at his chin, concentrating on his next set of words. "At the time, the crystals were of no consequence."

"But?"

"Earlier today, I got a 203. A man with a cut on his head. On a table next to the man, and on his person, I saw white crystals similar to the crystals seen at Duggan's case."

"That looked like salt or sugar?"

"It was salt."

"How do you know?"

"I tasted it."

"You did *what*?" Dewey frowned and sat back in his chair.

"I also tasted the crystals at Duggan's case. Also, salt."

"Coincidence?"

"Always a possibility. But this time, a few of the crystals were in the man's hair and his right ear. The other side of his face was lying on a table."

"How'd the salt get in his ear?"

"I don't know. I'm waiting for the coroner's report. I didn't say anything about Duggan's case and the salt to the coroner. No autopsy was done on Duggan's case. She was cremated."

"Did you say anything today?"

"No."

"You've seen both cases; do you think there's a connection?"

"I'm not sure." Luganos rose from his chair, smoothed the creases of his trousers and started to leave.

"Whoa, wait a minute! Why didn't you mention the crystals to the coroner?"

"I don't know; I didn't want to start any talk. You remember the last time we jumped the gun. The mayor went nuts. I'm waiting for a call from the coroner now."

Dewey frowned and nodded.

Back in his office, Luganos took a sip of coffee and opened the envelope that had just arrived from the coroner. He quickly flipped through the pages to the end of the report. What immediately caught his eye was the red circle around the value of the sodium and chloride concentrations in the blood and the comment, "Markedly abnormal."

Luganos stopped reading and dialed Dr. Giles's office. "This is Luganos. What happened to this guy?"

"What do you mean?"

"The sodium number."

"I knew you were bothered when you asked about doing toxicology. The white stuff on the deceased was salt—sodium chloride. The findings in the blood are bizarre, consistent with an injection of a concentrated salt solution."

Luganos sat forward. "Did you find an injection site?"

"You didn't read the report; I mentioned it twice."

"Is this murder?"

"No question, by salt injection."

Luganos hung up the phone and walked swiftly back to Dewey's office.

"Do you have something?" Dewey motioned to the chair in front of his desk.

"The autopsy report is consistent with murder by salt injection."

"Salt injection!" Dewey leaned back in his chair, clasping his hands behind his head. "That's a new one. Are you thinking serial?"

"Possibly, but we've got nothing except two deaths, one body, and an abnormal finding of salt in one victim's blood."

"Any mention of salt in the first case?"

"It wasn't documented."

"If it's serial, it looks like someone wants to play," said Dewey.

"You mean the salt?"

"What else could it mean?"

"I don't know what it means." Luganos stood up to leave.

"What about the commissioner and the press?"

Luganos focused his attention on the window behind Dewey's left shoulder. A blue jay had just landed on the sill. "Not yet; we really don't have anything."

Luganos walked out and headed back to his office, deep in thought. He sank into his desk chair and looked at the picture of his father. "Be a smart policeman," his father told him a month before he died. "You are Greek, and you are bright." His father was right; he had noticed the salt in Duggan's case. If it weren't for him, that detail would have been completely missed along with the connection to the second murder. *Being Greek is an advantage*, he thought to himself.

Luganos looked at the picture of his father and smiled. *What a handsome face.* He'd never had enough time with this wonderful man. His father was his hero, a man of action, always moving fast, talking on the phone, or getting ready to take another trip. Luganos moved closer to the picture, admiring his father's flawless skin. But he was different from his father. He was Slower moving, methodical, and interested in detail. He noticed odd things that others seem to miss.

Luganos remembered how proud his father was when he attended his promotion ceremony to detective. Later he, his father, and his uncle Nick went out for drinks, and his father said, "I always knew you were keen by the way you put together facts."

Luganos had few friends growing up, preferring to be by himself. Although handsome like his father, he developed bad acne in his early teens and that kept him shy of girls well into his twenties. He read a lot in high school, mostly detective mysteries: Agatha Christie, Raymond Chandler, C. K. Chesterton, and Sherlock Holmes. He was overjoyed when he discovered the famous Greek detectives series of Costas Haritos and Nick Stefanos.

Unlike his father, he felt socially uncomfortable in crowds. He didn't like foolish humor and preferred being formal and serious. He didn't care if some thought him skeptical and rigid; he was a superior detective and that's what mattered. Luganos turned on his computer and typed in the word "salt."

∞

Christian's telephone rang on the last notes of the first canon of Bach's *Goldberg Variations*, spoiling, for him, a moment of musical ecstasy.

"Hello?"

"Sorry, I hear the music, so excuse the interruption. Today I learned something that might interest you."

Christian was happy to hear the voice of his dear friend Brice. "I'm listening."

"I had lunch with Dewey at my old precinct." There was a pause. "He mentioned that someone is killing people with salt injections."

"Are you serious?"

"I am, but Christian, it's still hush-hush. I'm not supposed to talk about it."

"I've never heard of that before."

"I knew you'd be excited."

"A salt killer. Shit!" What immediately flashed through Christian's mind were stories of the Spanish Inquisition's practice of bathing a victim's feet with brine and then allowing goats to lick the feet until the flesh was gone.

"Anything else?"

"Christian, I've already said too much. But, yes, Dewey said there might be more than one victim."

"You've got to keep me informed."

"I will. How about dinner tomorrow?"

"Sounds good, at six?"

"Havana?"

"Great."

As soon as Christian hung up the phone, he realized he'd made no connections between salt and murder in his manuscript. In fact, he couldn't bring to mind a single instance when salt was used as a murder weapon. He had, of course, given examples from the Bible describing how salt was depicted as a symbol of curse, citing a verse from The Wisdom of Sirach, which read, "As God turns fresh water into salt so the heathen will experience his wrath." Also, he'd referenced Lot's wife being turned into a pillar of salt after looking back in defiance of the angel. Likewise, he'd quoted how God turned the land into a salt marsh because of the wickedness of the people, and, yes, he'd even covered how Barbarossa had demolished Milan and salted the streets and fields so nothing would grow. *Good old Brice,* he thought. *Always coming up with something new.*

Elijah Brice had been Christian's friend and mentor since Christian entered high school. From their first meeting, Christian considered Brice the most interesting man he'd ever met. Even now, as a retired NYPD detective, Brice spent his time rereading the classics and giving a weekly music appreciation/self-improvement class for incarcerated men at Rikers.

Brice had told him he was born in St. Thomas, the Virgin Islands, had lost both parents as an infant, and was raised by nuns in a home for orphaned boys, where he learned grammar, math, and the piano. When he was twenty, he came to the city on a music scholarship, but after one year, he decided to enter the Police Academy.

They met when Christian was fourteen and started playing baseball with the Police Athletic League. Brice was a volunteer coach. Their friendship came at just the right time. Brice was unmarried, childless, and lonely; Christian was struggling in a difficult relationship with his stepfather. Brice quickly became Christian's buddy, teaching him how to hit a fastball and how to punctuate a sentence.

Just about this time, Christian began listening to Be-Bop and the change that jazz was going through. Brice, a little stuffy, was slow to grasp this avant-garde form, but Christian loaned Brice several records, introducing him to Charlie Parker, Bud Powell, and Sonny Rollins. Their friendship flourished. One Sunday, Brice took Christian to his first classical concert. The Berlin Philharmonic was on tour in New York, doing a series of the Beethoven symphonies. Brice chose the Fifth, and Christian was hooked. Two weeks later they saw Rosalyn Tureck perform book one of Bach's *Well-Tempered Clavier*. After that they met several times a month to listen together and talk about music and life.

Brice was a big man, dark brown with light-gray eyes. His chest was wide like a Roman gladiator's, but he was soft-spoken; always knowing exactly what to say, as if he'd been trained to be eloquent. He took time to think before he answered questions. Christian studied these traits and vowed he would be like Brice when he grew up.

10

From the beginning, good things have been created for the good, just as evils have been created for the sinners. The elements needed for man's life are water and fire and salt.

– THE WISDOM OF SIRACH

HAVANA WAS A SMALL Manhattan restaurant three quarters of the way down a funny-shaped street joining Sixth Avenue with Bleeker Street. Inside, the tables were close together, giving the space a cozy feeling. The menu was Cuban, and the smell of black beans permeated the walls, upon which oil paintings of post-Castro Cuba were colorfully displayed.

Brice arrived first and ordered the house wine, the white bean soup, and the *ropa vieja*. Christian arrived soon after.

"You look tired," Brice said, folding his large hands in front of him.

"The deadline for the manuscript is close, and I've got a lot to finish; besides, there's shit at the hospital. But first tell me about our salt killer."

"Not much to tell. Dewey mentioned it as something unusual but said it was confidential."

"He said there could be multiple victims?"

"He did, but nothing else."

Christian tasted his margarita, then licked his top lip to savor the residue of salt left from the glass. He shook his head. "I've never heard of salt being used as a murder weapon."

Brice rubbed his hands together and thinned his eyes. "How did you get interested in something so *peculiar* as salt? It seems a little dull to me."

Christian smiled; he'd been asked that question many times, and usually by people he didn't care to engage.

"For a nephrologist, a precise understanding of how salt works in health and disease is basic. To understand how salt works in the body, one must know the kidney. During my senior year in med school, I gave a talk on salt and its relation to blood pressure and became fascinated."

"Everybody knows something about salt and health. You think the general public wants to read about that stuff?"

"That's just it. It's not the medical stuff that intrigued me; it's the other stuff."

"What other stuff?"

Christian took another sip, savoring the pleasing mix of salt and tequila, then pointed a finger at Brice. "Salt as a mysterious substance."

"A mysterious what?"

"The early alchemists believed salt had magical powers. They equated it with the four prime elements—earth, water, wind, and fire—and named it the fifth element. Why? It was salt's *immunity* against decay—the antiseptic power that prevents things from rotting. It was assumed that rotting and decay was the work of the Devil. And anything that prevented decay was a remedy against the devil. Salt was then assumed to be a charmed substance, even sacred. It was thought to be a symbol of incorruptibility, permanence, and durability. You must of have heard of a 'covenant of salt,' an agreement made with the binding tasting of salt. The agreement can never be altered or broken; it is forever permanent." Christian paused and ordered the oxtail, white rice, and black beans.

"According to Philo," he continued, "salt acts as a preservative to our bodies and our souls—like it does with meat and fish—and causes body and soul to escape corruption. The fascinating thing is that in *all* ages, and in *all* parts of the world, salt became invested with a significance far exceeding its natural properties.

"Medically, our need for it is so strong that our tongue is specifically designed to detect it, and not surprising, all our body fluids—blood, sweat, tears, urine, and, yes, semen—are loaded with it.

"The funny thing is, in severe disease of the heart, the liver, and the kidneys, the body loses its ability to control salt. Then it becomes a toxin that attacks us and slowly accumulates, combines with water, and refuses to be excreted; eventually killing us from salt and water overload. Life, it would seem, depends on how we handle this mysterious element: health-giving on the one hand, certain death on the other. It is sometimes called the ambivalent substance: health enhancing most of the time; deadly at other times."

"Wow," said Brice, setting down his fork. "Sounds like you've got something with the book. Hey, you could write a whole chapter on this creep if they ever catch him." Brice smiled and finished his drink.

Christian also smiled. "The book is for the general public. It's not pedantic and it isn't filled with science and medical advice, but with exotic and mystical details about this curious gift from the sea."

Christian drained his glass, raised his hand, and ordered more drinks.

11

Salt is good: But if the salt has lost its saltiness, wherewith will ye season it? Have salt in yourselves and have peace one with another.

~ MARK 9:50

CHRISTIAN LEANED BACK on the worn leather sofa and studied the smiling angels encased in plaster and caught in flight on the ceiling above.

Years ago, this place was the nun's dining room. It was an elegant space of dark-paneled wood, immaculate white tablecloths, and settings of four at each of its five tables. A slender vase with a delicate rose, sometimes red, sometimes white, sat in the center of each table. The air in the room was always fresh and filled with the hint of roses. When the Sisters of Charity lost control of the hospital, the room was converted into a doctor's lounge. The walls were then refinished with plasterboard and metal coat hooks. Now, the room smelled of stale cigarettes, cheap coffee, used Styrofoam cups, and old newspapers scattered across several dilapidated leather sofas.

Save for a quick phone call, Christian seldom entered this room. Each time he did, sorrow filled his chest as he remembered how it used to be when the graceful sisters took their meals here. Christian loved the nuns, remembering how they befriended him right from the beginning of his training. Medical school didn't teach empathy, but at Mercy he was impressed by the way the nuns cared for all the patients regardless of race, station, or wealth, with love and kindness.

Christian left the lounge and entered a side corridor that led to the old nursing school adjacent to the hospital. This dark passageway, rarely used these days, remained spooky with its dim ceiling lights; it was now a resting place for statues that once stood as sentinels to the old wards before the renovation.

He arrived outside Father Joseph's office and stopped to read the sign written in dark magic marker: "Knock before entering."

Christian knocked and entered.

A woman stood in the center of the room, poised with a dark Dominican-tan and jet-black hair. Her subtle fragrance greeted him, and the dim office lights played off her pearls and the creases of her white silk blouse.

"Good Morning, Dr. Christian, I'm Mara."

She smiled, making deliberate eye contact, and it flashed through his mind that they had met before. But where? He hadn't seen her in the hospital, or he would have certainly remembered. She offered her hand diplomatically, a soft touch. She smiled reassuringly, and her perfume struck him as familiar.

"Father Joseph is waiting; please go right in."

Christian felt the beat in his temple as he read the sign on the priest's office door: "Knock once, then enter."

He knocked and entered.

The cleric, seated at his desk, looked up and smiled—forced and practiced, self-assured. His slender face, closely shaven with patches of razor burn, and offset with pale blue eyes, was striking. The blinds at the windows were closed; the only light came from a bright desk lamp.

With a slight wave of his hand, he motioned to Christian to take the chair in front of his desk. Christian noticed a "No Smoking" sign on the wall behind the man in black.

The priest closed an open folder.

"You've done well, Dr. Christian. Tell me, was it difficult at the beginning?" Father Joseph adjusted himself in his seat and widened his eyes in anticipation.

"To what are you referring?" Christian folded his arms, prepared for a list of what had now become familiar questions, no doubt concerning overcoming life's struggles as a Black man.

"Being the only minority back then." The priest reopened the folder in front of him. "Weren't you the first person of color to come through this program?"

"The second in medicine and the first in kidney diseases."

The priest smiled, tightly this time, as if holding something back. "Dr. Forsyth, bless his soul—always moving forward, always taking chances, and always ahead of his time. I couldn't tell when I first looked at your picture. I suspect training under those circumstances was still somewhat of a challenge?"

"Residency is always a challenge." Christian unfolded his arms.

"Come now, Dr. Christian, be truthful, you must have known you were being held to a different—more likely higher—standard."

"I suppose so, but it didn't interfere with my work." A pause. "And I am being truthful," Christian added, offering no smile. He interlocked the fingers of his hands and made direct eye contact with the man behind the desk.

The priest leaned forward. "Oh, don't mind me, Doctor, I'm just trying to get a read on you. My training is in psychology, and I'm always interested in learning how people adapt to challenging situations. Doctor Greenberg says you run an excellent section and have the pulse of the institution. I'm always on the lookout for talent, those who've done well in rough waters. Still, however, I like to make my own assessments. Dr. Greenberg says I can rely on whatever you tell me. Are you engaged in research?"

"Yes."

"How many publications in the last five years?"

"Three papers in peer-reviewed journals."

"Anything else?"

"A book in the making."

"Busy, I see."

Father Joseph leaned back in his chair, clicking the gold ring on his index finger against the ornate silver crucifix that rested on his chest. "May I ask you a personal question that you can decline to answer?"

"Certainly."

"How do you feel about God?" Father Joseph's smile became wider.

"I'm frightened of him."

"Good." The priest nodded approval. "Now let's get down to business."

Christian quickly reviewed the salient points of the teaching program, the recent accomplishments of the full-time faculty, and the hospital's new community-outreach programs.

An hour later, he closed the door to Father Joseph's office. Mara had left, but her fragrance lingered, creating, this time, a visceral sensation he couldn't explain.

As Christian made his way back to the main hospital, he wondered if the words "person of color" rather than "African American" had any significance. Person of color was, of course, softer and more sophisticated, but always made him think of "a person of interest."

Father Joseph looked to be in his fifties. He was Irish, certainly, and came just short of having a cruel twist to his mouth. He was a fast learner and wasn't shy about asking provocative questions. This man was an experienced examiner and a careful listener; in religious circles, that meant power—someone not to be taken lightly.

When Christian opened the door to the main hospital, encountering the noise and hectic scene, he stopped, put the palm of his hand to his nose, and revisited Mara's scent. Licorice, maybe anise? He smiled, realizing where they had first met: in the dark of Crystal's bedroom. Now he understood how Crystal knew about the hospital's financial mess.

Later that night, Christian sat at his desk, reviewing his talk with Father Joseph. He smiled to himself, thinking he should have told the priest why his residency had been challenging. It had had little to do with learning the fundamentals of medicine; it was that Christian had more to think about than medicine. For instance, was his hair cut and combed *just right*? Was his uniform spotless, and were his notes precise? Was he articulate? And yes, he'd had to be careful not to be too chummy with the White nurses (and they were all White back then) or linger at their stations too long. And who would be the attending physician this month or next; would they have some unease about him as a trainee? What about the patients? How did they feel having a Black doctor touch their tummy? And what of those first few seconds after he entered a new patient's room and watched their facial expression as they tried to figure out his background: mixed-Black, Hispanic, or what?

All in all, he seldom encountered any specific instance during his training that he could say was racist. The attendings were great mentors, the patients were respectful, and so were his fellow trainees. The nuns were unbelievably kind. But it was his social identity and his life experiences to that point that made him feel he was different, like he was being watched. So even in a place that was almost devoid of racial tensions, his mind was programed to feel like the *other*. And like the *other*, he was burdened with having to constantly think about what people thought of his otherness.

12

*Prince Henry: O, that there were some virtue
in my tears, that might relieve you!
King John: The salt in them is hot.*

– SHAKESPEARE, KING JOHN (ACT V)

RUPERT OPENED HIS EYES and felt a steel numbness in his left arm. He'd fallen asleep in an awkward position, and the normal sensation of touch had not yet returned. Another sign that he was dying.

He slipped out of bed, walked to the window, and inhaled the eucalyptus plant on the sill. Its sharp aroma quickly cleared his palate and taste buds. For a correct calculation, his tongue and nose must be cleared of any fugitive distractions.

In the bathroom, as he emptied his bladder, he placed his index finger into his stream of urine. He then tasted his finger. Rupert, like other humans, discovered the saltiness of his body by licking his skin, or tasting his tears. But, in addition, he discovered that by sampling his urine, tasting it, he could measure his constant salt loss. In his struggle to stay alive, he'd trained his tongue to revert to its primitive function as a salt seeker and, in his case, a calculator. Rupert believed that when God takes away a gift, he always leaves a new one behind.

Rupert's life depended on the delicate balance between intake and loss. And tasting his urine—this unusual intimacy—helped him to avoid the painful needles that had traumatized him as a child.

In normal beings, the kidneys control the body's salt by either absorbing it back into the bloodstream or discarding it into the urine. But not so for Rupert: his kidneys were neutered by nature, made useless and unable to save his body's salt. Now his tongue, with its evolutionary potential, replaced his kidneys, monitored his body's salt loss, and guided his daily replacement of this indispensable requirement for his life. After determining the salt content of his urine, he took the equivalent replacement in salt-rich bouillon soup.

Rupert selected a blue blazer, gray slacks, white shirt, and red-and-blue-striped tie. He also chose the black, thick-soled loafers, as they made him an inch taller. After placing several salt tablets in his pocket and putting on sunglasses, he decided to walk some of the way, partly to enjoy the summer day, but also to test his stamina. Recently, he'd noticed intermittent shortness of breath and weakness in his calves with any sustained exertion.

Sixth Avenue was overflowing with activity—the neighborhood down-and-outs, the foreign tourists: Germans, Scandinavians, Spanish, and Asians with their oversized cameras and wide, sun-blocking hats. He easily recognized the American out-of-towners, talking loudly and stretching their necks like geese, peering up at street signs, taking pictures with their small cameras.

When he reached Thirty-Fourth Street, he was exhausted and both legs were almost numb. He hailed a taxi the rest of the way to the Academy of Medicine. There, he picked up two papers on statistics that he needed to use in the study he was conducting.

From the Academy, he took another taxi to the Seminary at Morningside Heights, where he requested a rare religious volume and took notes for two hours. At six-thirty, he looked at his watch and realized he'd have to leave to be on time for his shift at St. Mary's as night-nurse administrator, which started at 7:15 p.m.

∞

St. Mary's was a small one-hundred-bed hospital on West Fifty-Fourth Street and Eighth Avenue. Rupert sat in his office there under the halo of the desk lamp, reviewing the complaints he'd collected to date. After an hour of complicated calculations, he threw his pencil to the floor, realizing the sample size of his study population was too small. No conclusions could be made, and he would need more cases. He closed his notes and rested his eyes.

As he drifted into slumber, the Voice became agitated and started spewing disconnected words. First, it recited Newton's Three Laws of Motion. Then, it called plays like a quarterback in T-formation, and finally, in the deep voice of a Black Baptist preacher with a white handkerchief to his drenched face, it shouted a frenzied: *Thank God and have mercy, 'cause Heeee changed our nature of dust and made us the salt of the truth and rescued us, lest we become the prey of the serpent!* The Voice screamed, *Have Mercy!* in a James Brown squeal, waking Rupert to the shrill sound of his hospital beeper. He dialed the extension.

"This is Mr. Pike. What's up?"

"It's Katy Chin on Med Two. We have a real asshole down here, refusing to lower the volume of his TV. He's a druggie who came in yesterday with bronchitis, and now he's asking for more pain meds. He's going wild, wants to speak to an administrator."

"What's his name?"

"Johnson."

"I'll be right down."

∞

Anfony Salim Johnson had been admitted to the hospital the night before with a severe cough and delirium. His urine tested positive for cocaine. By early morning, his mental status had completely cleared, but he vehemently denied using drugs. He was started on antibiotics when he coughed up yellow mucous and was advised to stay another twenty-four hours. Now he complained of muscular pain from his coughing. In reading Johnson's chart, Rupert found four entries describing the use of profane language since Johnson had been admitted to the hospital.

Rupert walked into the patient's room.

"Mr. Johnson, I'm Mr. Pike, the night nurse administrator."

Johnson, a short, stern-looking Black man with an earring and a shaved head, did not look in Rupert's direction. His TV was blasting. Rupert tried again.

"The nurse said that you're refusing to lower the volume of your TV."

"She full o'shit!" Johnson shouted the words clearly with an effeminate overlay.

"Mr. Johnson, there's no need for that type of language."

"Look, man, there ain't no earphones in this joint, and I can't hear shit when the TV is low. You know what I'm saying?"

"I'm sorry that we've run out of earphones, but you must lower the volume."

"Look, man, I hurt, and I need mo' pain pills." Johnson raised himself from a prone position and stared at Rupert. "Did you hear what I said, man? I need another pill for my pain."

"I'll page the physician on call, but you must lower the volume on the TV before I leave the floor."

"Don't tell me what to do, man." Johnson was small and muscular. His shiny head gleamed in the overhead fluorescent lights, and his bushy beard, encircling his mouth, exaggerated the size of his teeth, giving him a fierce expression.

"Mr. Johnson, if you don't lower the volume, I'll call security, and they'll turn off the television power or escort you out of the hospital."

"Fuck you, and fuck security," Johnson said calmly, wiggling his head as spoke. He turned off the TV and threw the remote to the floor.

As Rupert left the room, Johnson yelled, "I want to file a fucking complaint!"

Rupert stopped and turned to the patient, a smile on his face. "That's your right, Mr. Johnson. I'll be back with the forms."

The Voice began mimicking Johnson's confident street dialect, cursing in vulgar fashion and ending with a litany from an old Greek papyrus: *A little boy must eat bread, nibble salt, and not touch the sauce, but if he asks for wine, give him your knuckles.*

13

For everyone shall be salted with fire, and every sacrifice shall be salted with salt.

~ MARK 9:49

ANFONY JOHNSON WAS A SPECIAL type of addict—a "snorter" to be exact. He neither mainlined nor skin-popped. Desperately frightened of needles and absolutely vain about scars on his skin, he sucked drugs up his nose. First powdered pills, then cocaine—the latter after he discovered he liked sleeping with both women *and* men, but not at the same time. He existed as a functional addict: unemployed, on public assistance, using cocaine daily, and, whenever possible, peddling stolen goods.

Two days after Johnson left the hospital, Rupert called him.

"Your dime," Johnson answered.

"Mr. Johnson, I represent St. Mary's Hospital."

"Yeah."

"I'm calling about the complaint you recently filed at the hospital."

"Yeah, I was just thinking about that. I'm still pissed."

"Your complaint has been reviewed, and the hospital is prepared to reimburse you for your hardship and inconvenience."

"You mean money?"

"Well, yes, but I need a little more information before we can send a check."

"What I gotta do?"

"This must be strictly confidential; the hospital doesn't like publicity. We should meet so I can finish the paperwork. When can we do that?"

Rupert jotted down Johnson's address, scheduled a visit, then hung up the phone. *How many times have I met fuckers like this, who fill their God-given body with poison, then cry for help? They squeeze on the plump nipple of society and suck out the juice. Too many patients want something to get high. If you say no, they show their animal side. I know; I take the complaints.*

Rupert knew Johnson's mindset; the mere hint of getting something for nothing—of beating the system—would be enough. The day Johnson left the hospital, the housekeeping division reported four new bedsheets missing along with three rolls of toilet paper. And later that evening, the nursing station reported a gross of number-ten-gauge syringes with their needles missing, items that were highly sought after by the druggies on the street.

∞

Johnson's building was on the Lower East Side—shabby but not destitute. The social worker's note said that he needed to live on the ground floor because he couldn't climb stairs. The Voice muttered: *Can you believe that bullshit?*

After one ring, Johnson flung open the door, smiling, unsteady, eyes glazed over. "You from the hospital?"

"Yes, Mr. Johnson."

"Come in."

The apartment was small: a one-room kitchenette and a tiny bathroom with a sliding curtain as its door. A small cot with a thin mattress took up half of the space. The room had two chairs, one oversized with brown puffy pillows that looked as if it had once been rained on, and the other, a green canvas beach chair with paint stain in the seat. One wall had a section of shelves stacked with odd objects: an old camera, an outdated film projector, a small black-and-white TV, and several worn backpacks. The place smelled of cat litter.

"Didn't I meet you before?" Johnson squinted through his fog, still unsteady on his feet.

"I don't think so, Mr. Johnson."

"Man, I was sick. I just remember some dude talking to me like I was a piece of shit." Rupert sat in the bulky chair, and Johnson sat on the cot.

"I've brought us tea."

"Thanks, man. I'm real thirsty." Johnson drank the entire cup in one gulp, then gave a loud whistle. From beneath the cot, a large gray cat with green eyes emerged and stretched, walked in a circle, then bumped against Johnson's leg.

Rupert watched as Johnson caressed the cat's head. The animal stood on his hind legs and pawed at Johnson's knees. After several strokes along the cat's back, Johnson's arms fell to his sides, and he rested back on the cot. He was asleep and snoring.

As Rupert searched for a vein, the friendly animal looked on with a serious expression. After the injection, Rupert gently petted the cat, washed his hands. He then spread the salt while the Voice recited from Saint Chromatius: *And so, just as salt, when it works in any flesh does not allow corruption, carries off bad odors, drives out filth, and does not allow worms.*

Before he left, Rupert removed an envelope from his breast pocket, opened it, and placed a note on the canvas beach chair with the paint stain in the center.

The Voice whispered: *Let's have a little fun.*

14

I saw the salt
In this shaker
In the salt flat,
I know
You will never believe me
but it sings
the salt sings.

~ PABLO NERUDA

EARLIER IN THE EVENING, Luganos had entertained a young woman from Greece—a student at Pace University who'd just turned twenty-one. The student's older sister, a former intimate friend of Luganos, asked him to help find her sister a job. He did find her a nice part-time position. After a time a friendship developed, and now they were regularly having sex. After she left, he was exhausted and remained in bed.

∞

At 10 p.m., Luganos's phone rang. Still half asleep, he answered on the second ring.

"This is Dewey. He's done it again."

"What?"

"He's killed a druggie; same MO. The guy's friend next-door, another druggie, needed sugar and came in through a fire escape window. This time there was a note."

"A note?" Luganos rubbed his eyes, aware of the balmy smell of sex on his hands.

"Giles is on the scene now. Valdez took the call; I'm giving it to you."

"I'll leave now."

"Call me when you get there."

∞

Members of the crime-scene unit and the coroner's office were in the apartment when Luganos arrived. The next-door neighbor, still under the influence of some hallucinogen, told Luganos he'd discovered the body. He said he climbed through the window and saw someone walk through the wall. Before he was released, he asked if he could care for the cat because he didn't want the animal to end up in a glue factory.

The body was slumped on the cot; salt crystals were on the victim's skin and clothes. Giles walked over to Luganos and pointed to the note.

"I can't make much sense of it, but I think it's your buddy."

"I agree."

Luganos stepped into the bathroom and rang Dewey. "The same MO," he confirmed, covering his mouth to conceal his conversation.

"What about the note?"

"Biblical mumbo jumbo."

A long pause followed. Dewey cleared his throat. "I'm asking someone outside the department for help."

"Oh," said Luganos, unease in his voice.

"He's a medical doctor, some kind of salt expert. Brice told me about him."

"Do you think it's wise to involve an outsider at this stage—I mean before we've had a chance to get a handle on things?"

"If I didn't think it was wise, I wouldn't have suggested it. Trust me. This is going to be a tough one. My office, at nine."

Luganos walked back toward the room where the deceased lay. He fingered his chin, the painful area he'd irritated from his activities earlier that evening. He flipped two Tums into his mouth, regretting not having taken his miracle pill before leaving his apartment. A tinge of anger dried his mouth as he thought to himself, *What the fuck could a salt expert tell us about murder? The note clearly shows the killer wants to jerk us around.*

He then methodically reviewed the crime scene and made more notes.

15

*The nature of salt is fixed by means of water,
the heat of the sun, and the blowing of
the wind: and from that which it was,
it is made into another species.*

~ CHROMATIUS, CORRESPONDENT TO AMBROSE

AFTER THE CALL FROM DEWEY, Christian found it difficult to sleep; nevertheless, he was out of bed by 6 a.m. After going to the bathroom, he knelt on his soft exercise pad and did twenty slow, deliberate push-ups. He followed with thirty uninterrupted, quick dual-bicep curls with five-pound weights, and an additional fifteen slow push-ups. In the bathroom, he brushed his teeth, shaved, and showered. He chose a blue suit, white shirt, and burgundy tie. At 7 a.m., he dialed the dialysis unit and spoke to Crystal, checking to see if she had any questions before he left his apartment.

Normally, if he were not assigned to Father Joseph, he would have teaching rounds at ten o'clock, a noon conference, a three o'clock meeting with the research fellows, and a four o'clock medical student presentation. But not today.

Christian was flattered when he received Dewey's call but somewhat anxious; he'd never done anything like this before. There was no denying: he was absolutely intrigued by the salt killer. Shit, could you believe someone was killing people with salt at the exact time he was writing a book about this intriguing substance. The timing was amazing. Wouldn't it be something if he could incorporate these murders into his book to show the fascinating symbolism of salt as a mysterious and spooky substance?

Christian was uncomfortably aware that his interest was with the murderer and his method of killing, and not the victims as it should be. The story was too good. He shook his head, trying to get rid of the guilt.

Who could do this? No ordinary person. And do the police expect me to help them catch a killer?

Christian wondered, from his life's experiences, how the police would react to him. He knew, at the very least, they would be surprised. They'd say—no, they'd *think*—"Who is this Black guy?" He knew that Blackness carried a stigma. Even now, when he entered a patient's room, the family often reacted, ever so slightly, in those first few seconds. He knew what they were thinking: *Is this guy really the chief? He's Black; damn, he must be smart!* Or: *Shit, this guy is Black!* And often, before he'd left the patient's room, someone, well-meaning of course, would say that he reminded them of David Dinkins, a former mayor; or Gregory Hines, a dancer; or, just as likely, a fair-skinned Black sports figure.

Christian ate a bowl of Cheerios and milk, took ten milligrams of Lipitor, and left the house at eight-fifteen.

∞

"I'm Chief Detective Dewey, and this is Detective Luganos. Thank you, Doctor, for coming in today. Please have a seat."

Dewey settled behind his desk and nodded to Luganos to proceed. The room was painted a dismal green, and the windows needed cleaning. The wall behind Dewey's desk was filled with pictures, letters, and awards. One picture showed Dewey and Brice receiving a silver plaque. Christian took a seat in front of Dewey's desk.

Luganos shifted in his chair to face Christian but did not raise his eyes from a stack of three-by-five index cards. "Over the past several weeks, two—and possibly three—homicides have occurred. The last two victims were injected with a salt solution, confirmed by the coroner's office. In each case, common salt was sprinkled over the victim. The third murder took place last night. This time the killer left a note."

Dewey handed Christian a copy of the note.

> *By my own body, I know this to be true.*
>
> *All things prove good for the Godly, just as they turn into evil for the sinful.*
>
> *And so, these shall inhabit a parched place in the wilderness, a salt land not inhabited.*
>
> *They have broken their covenant, but having made mine, I cannot.*

"Any thoughts, Doctor?" Dewey turned on his desktop tape recorder.

"In what respect?"

"In any respect," said Luganos, his eyes still on the index cards.

Christian read the note for the second time and then looked up. He was aware that Luganos had not yet raised his head to recognize him. He remembered Brice's warning that outside consultants were not always welcomed.

"Lethal administration of salt is rare. Most often, it's a mistake made in hospitals. What we have here is obviously deliberate. Besides his knowledge of salt, the killer is no stranger to the Bible. 'All these things prove good for the Godly, just as they turn into evil for the sinful' is a quote from the book of Ecclesiastics. My hunch is there's a deeper meaning to the murder."

"You're familiar with the phrase?" asked Dewey.

"Yes."

"What does it mean?"

"I'm not certain what it means here, but the ancients believed in the ambivalent nature of salt and its dual identity—a sign of goodwill or fellowship for the good, or, conversely, a curse for the evil." Christian rested back in his chair.

"Please continue, Doctor," said Dewey, leaning in over his desk.

"The second part of the note, 'And so these shall inhabit the parched places in the wilderness,' is a biblical reference from Jeremiah. I think it goes, 'He who departs from God's service shall inhabit a parched land, a salt land, not inhabited.'"

Christian saw Luganos lift his eyes from his cards and focus on a point just above Christian's head.

"He sounds like a religious nut," said Dewey.

Luganos sighed and directly engaged Christian's eyes. "Do you think he could be a scholar, say, like yourself?"

Christian frown and thought to himself *Wow! 'Someone like yourself.' What did that mean?* "I suppose so, but I'm certain that you've already considered that the use of salt points to a number of occupations and professions, including cooks, chemists, and even men of the cloth."

"Yes we're looking into that, Doctor." Luganos lowered his eyes back to his cards. Dewey left his chair and walked to the window. "We are in the beginning stages of our investigation, which involves a thorough background check on the victims and the forensics in the last murder. Do you have any other suggestions?"

Christian loosened the top button of his jacket. "Nothing other than that our man may be fixated on salt and the Bible."

"You said, 'our man,'" Luganos interrupted. "On what grounds?" His mouth was twisted into a half-smile, more like a half-sneer.

"Maybe you should disregard that answer completely."

"I already have," Luganos said, fingering his chin again. "Couldn't it be a woman, Doctor?"

"Yes, I suppose it could be." Christian immediately wished he'd not speculated. Luganos smiled. Dewey gave Luganos a long side-glance. Luganos looked toward the ceiling, still touching his irritated chin.

"Could our person of interest just be a cold-blooded killer?" Luganos raised his voice slightly. "Could all the rest of this—the salt and the note—be pure bullshit? Some smart-ass trying to make us think he's spooky or crazy with religion?" Luganos got up out of his chair and looked down at Christian, smiling.

"That's also possible," said Christian. "But whomever it is, the use of salt in combination with the references make me think it's someone unusual."

"Unusual in what sense, Doctor?" asked Luganos, still smiling.

"Quoting from the scriptures that relate to salt in this setting requires a bit of sophistication."

"You mean all of this couldn't be bogus?" Luganos spread his arms apart to emphasize his point. "You do know, or you should know, that crooks, politicians, and especially killers, lie and fake shit all the time. So, I repeat: Could this be bogus? Some weirdo, not nuts or spooky, just trying to keep us occupied with salt hocus-pocus and a little biblical bullshit thrown in on the side?"

"Anything is possible, but I would say that salt has its own strange history." Christian paused. "Whenever we encounter it, there's often symbolic significance lurking someplace. At one time, almost all of our human activities were influenced by it—especially curses. I've been writing about this, and that's why I suggest that we may be dealing with an unusual weirdo, if that's how you choose to characterize the murderer."

"Thank you, Doctor." Luganos reclined in his chair.

"Anything else, Doctor?" asked Dewey.

"The last lines are Old Testament."

"Is that important?" asked Luganos.

"Only in that some have suggested the God of the Old Testament is punishing and revenging, while the God of the New Testament is more forgiving and compassionate. I don't know if that's accurate. I don't have any religious credentials."

Luganos leaned forward in his chair, close to Christian's face. "Are there any *other* implications of Old Testament versus New Testament?"

"No, but the killer sounds angry." Christian buttoned his jacket and sat back in his chair. "Historically, salting, if that's what this represents, was a deed of anger. The Romans, after defeating Carthage, salted the city because of their disdain for the African general Hannibal, who almost brought Rome to her knees. The Romans didn't want anything to grow in that land again. Salting is an act of strong hostility toward the person or thing salted. In religious writings, seriousness is implied when salt is mentioned. Could that be a clue to the motive of the killer?"

"Any further comments, Doctor?" asked Dewey.

"The killer uses the word 'these.' Does that mean the victims have something in common; maybe that they're related in some way?"

"So far, there's nothing to suggest that the victims have anything in common," interjected Luganos, annoyance in his tone.

Dewey placed his large hands flat on his desk as if to do a push-up. "Looks like we got a real problem here; lots of fucking angles, and maybe a smart-ass killer or psycho or both.

Dewey leaned back, his chair making a loud squeak. He turned to Christian. "This has been very instructive, and I'd like you to work with us on this, if that's possible." Dewey's tone was polite, a measured smile on his face. "I'm certain we can work out some form of compensation."

"I don't think I can make a formal commitment; I'm under strict time constraints; the new academic year has just begun. I'll try to help if I can; in any event, no compensation is necessary."

Dewey turned to Luganos. "Do you want to add anything?"

"We're in the initial stages of the investigation, and I'd emphasize that all of this is confidential and should not be discussed outside of this room."

Christian looked at Luganos, who was still looking straight ahead, then replied, "Understood."

16

You will realize how salt is the taste of another man's bread, and how hard the blisters are when going up and down other people's stairs.

~ DANTE

CHRISTIAN RECLINED BACK onto the soft white pillow and admired Crystal's ebony skin. She was beautiful. Seeing her exposed this way, he couldn't help think of her vulnerability because of her color, and of all the women who were stolen and consumed in the slave trade. He was aware that his two aunts, both very dark in complexion, had fair skinned children, as did his mother, in their teens.

"Do you like the taste of my margarita?" he asked her.

"I do. And did you like what I just did?" She raised her eyes, then smiled and ran a finger over his lips.

"Yes, that was nice."

She raised her head from his chest, her nipples pointed, her breasts full and heavy. She picked up her drink, took a sip and licked the rim of her glass, spilling some of it on his chest. She sucked away what had spilled.

"You taste salty," she said.

"That's a compliment."

"Whoever thought of mixing tequila and salt to make a drink?"

"The drink was created in a bar in Suarez, Mexico, in 1950, by a Texan. Tequila comes from the fermented leaves of the agave plant and was chewed and stewed by the natives of Mexico centuries before the Spanish Conquest."

She rested back and placed a hand on his bare thigh. "What caused your divorce?" She patted him twice.

Christian pulled the sheet over both of them, signaling he would be serious.

"We should never have married. Everyone thought we were a great-looking couple. And that's what we were: a great-looking couple without a shred in common, except youthful sex. She was beautiful and had just started modeling for a Black magazine, and I was a promising student who wanted to be a doctor."

"What complexion was she?"

"Fair, like me." Christian wondered if he should have answered so truthfully.

"Was that part of it? I mean, the light skin?"

"Not consciously, then, but I don't know for sure. Whites, with their craziness about color have infected Blacks with that same craziness. My own stepfather looked down on dark complexion. I still remember how he described a person at his job he'd argued with. He said, "You know he was Black, black like tar; you know that evil-looking type."

"He was racist."

"Maybe."

"Did you have any children?"

"No, A miscarriage. And by that time, we had nothing in common, nothing to save. We came from different backgrounds, each with a load of shit that didn't make things easier. Christian leaned over and kissed her full lips, a slight taste of salt lingering. He pulled down the sheet and licked her belly and continued to move lower when she pulled his head back.

"Let's talk more."

Christian drained the last of his drink. "What about you?"

"Me? I came from a small village near a large river that overflowed every year. I lived in a one-story house with kerosene lamps and slept under mosquito netting. When I was twelve, my mother died in childbirth along with the baby, and my father left shortly after. I went to live with my aunt and her husband, and I became their house servant. Soon, my aunt's husband began sexually abusing me. Fortunately, he was sent to prison for killing the husband of a woman he'd been sleeping with. After that, I went to a Catholic school for orphaned girls, where I studied to be a nurse's aide. The Sisters of Charity served tours in Haiti; I was noticed and given a chance to study at Mercy through an exchange program. Then I learned there was a shortage of dialysis nurses in this country, and I could get a green card faster if I worked in that field. And here I am."

"And you and Mara?"

"When I was with my aunt and being abused, I hated men. When I went to the Catholic home for girls, all of us had been abused in one way or another. We needed affection and friendship. I fell in love with one of the girls and began being intimate with her. The sex was comforting and safe. It took time for me to realize that I also liked men." Crystal looked at him and smiled. "Does that bother you?"

"Obviously not. Do you have other male friends besides me?"

"That's none of your business. But, no, I have no other male friends."

"Do you ever think of marriage? Children?" he asked.

"No, and I don't want children. I like my life as it is; I'm happy. What do you want in life?"

"I want to finish this book and prove that I'm accomplished in more ways than one. I want to leave something artistic behind after I'm gone."

"You want to be a Renaissance man?"

"I would like that."

"Isn't salt a strange topic for a whole book? It doesn't seem that interesting."

Christian chuckled. "Maybe, but just today, the police asked me to help them using my knowledge about salt."

"For what?"

"I can't discuss it, but I know if things go right, it'll be great for my book."

"Be careful. In my country, we stay clear of the authorities. They can be as dangerous as the criminals."

Christian pulled her close and kissed her. She threw her head back, her eyes dreamy. She pushed him back onto the pillow and straddled him.

"Enough talk; your margarita has gotten to me." She reached behind herself and made a delicate adjustment. In response, he arched his back and took a deep breath.

17

And every grain offering of yours, you shall season with salt, so that the salt of the covenant of your God shall not be lacking from your grain offering; with all your offerings you shall offer salt.
- LEVITICUS 2:13

LUGANOS, DRIPPING WET, stepped from the shower, keeping his eyes on Anna's bottom as she delicately slipped into her panties.

He gave Anna two-hundred dollars a month for the time they spent together and her easy availability. For him, the arrangement could not be better: he, a bachelor in his fifties, and she, twenty-one, better-than-average-looking, and dearly in need of funds. Her only fault, he bemoaned, was the excessive body hair around her private area, which he'd politely asked her to modify. But, notwithstanding this minor shortcoming, and in light of her enthusiasm in bed, it was a good arrangement.

After Anna left, he sat dabbing his irritated chin with peroxide and replayed yesterday's meeting with Christian. It was obvious that Dewey liked the doctor and wanted him on the case. The doctor handled himself well: measured, understated, and polite. *But all fucking consultants were like that at the beginning.*

Luganos thought back to six months before, when they'd worked with another consultant who was to testify as an expert witness. They had the evidence to convict a drug lord for murder, and the case was going fine. The night before the consultant was to testify, he was arrested for soliciting sexual favors on Forty-Second Street, and the case was postponed for two days. When it resumed, the defense questioned the expert's recent arrest, implying he was of questionable character. Things went south, and they lost the case.

The more Luganos thought of having to tolerate Christian, the more aggrieved he felt. He remembered Christian's remark about Hannibal and Rome. Christian said Hannibal was an African general, but Luganos recalled seeing a movie in which Hannibal was White. He wondered whether Christian was one of those agitating Black guys who suggested that many important historical people were Black. Just the other night, Luganos saw a TV program that claimed the father of Alexander Dumas, the man who'd written *The Count of Monte Cristo* and *The Three Musketeers* was Black, as was Alexander Pushkin, the famous Russian poet. He could see that Christian was definitely mixed and wondered about his ethnic background. He shook his head as he began to dress. *How did this guy get interested in this historical stuff? Does he really believe all this shit about salt? This killer is clever; the salt is all a cover.*

18

No man is worth his salt who is not ready at all times to risk his well-being, to risk his body, to risk his life, in a great cause.

— THEODORE ROOSEVELT

THE HUMAN TONGUE, overflowing with its sensitive nerve endings is perfectly placed. This oral guardian scrutinizes all offerings before it accepts or rejects. The tapered tip is given to sweets, and the area just behind—a modest portion—is reserved for salt taste.

Rupert's tongue was sore—the tip and both sides. This new irritation, a cold sore-like burning, worried him. He placed a half-teaspoon of Xylocaine gel into a quarter glass of water, stirred, and then dipped his tongue into the pink liquid. Several minutes later, he returned to his bed, placed both hands comfortably behind his head, and hummed the opening notes of "We are climbing Jacob's ladder."

Outside the rain was falling. Rupert heard the drops beating on his windowpane and thought back to another rainy day. He'd been admitted to the hospital for a serious episode of salt loss. One day his mother arrived to visit wearing a bright print dress, a short tailored jacket, and new makeup. The sight of her frightened him, because she usually dressed in blue jeans and an old windbreaker. The dark lipstick gave her a scary look, and long eyelashes didn't fit. She carried a bag of potato chips she'd already opened, and made loud noises as she chewed.

"Are you going someplace?" he asked.

"Yes, sweetie." She looked away, avoiding his eyes. "The girls and me."

"Are you going today?"

"Kinda, but I brought you some goodies, so you won't feel bad."

Rupert smiled obligingly, knowing it was proper to be grateful when someone brought you a gift. But he felt bad.

"I'll only be gone tomorrow, and Auntie Helen will stop in. I'm going to Albany for a reunion."

She leaned closer, and he saw a hole in the armpit of her dress. Her stale breath, a mixture of tobacco and chips, forced him to turn his head as she kissed his cheek.

"Are you getting better?" she asked.

"Yes."

"I can't wait for to you grow out of this thing so you can be a normal boy."

"Momma, I'm getting normal."

That was the last time he saw his mother and the first time he heard the Voice.

Rupert was confused when the Voice initially appeared: he assumed it was his own thinking, but within a short time he distinguished his thoughts from that of the Voice. Rupert never spoke of this new visitor. He already had one serious medical fault and didn't want to add to his problem list. People already referred to him as "that sickly boy." In the beginning, of course, the Voice frightened him, but in time he looked forward to its visits.

Tell me again of your discovery, the Voice now broke in, tentative and ingratiating, softly interrupting the calm of the raindrops outside his window, bringing him back to the present.

"Oh," said Rupert, sitting up, pleased that the Voice was there. "As you remember, my illness declared itself at birth. Somehow, I survived despite the speculations of the learned doctors." Rupert smiled and a tear descended his cheek. "When I was old enough to realize what was happening to me—the constant poking for blood to check my salt level—I wished I were dead."

What about your mother?

"My mother?" Rupert pulled at his right ear and felt heat flooding his face. He cleared his throat. "My sickness was too much for her." Rupert licked the tear descending his cheek and tried to estimate its salt content. He could not; the zylocaine had dulled the nerve endings in his tongue.

"The state sent me to Dunsmoor, an institution that cared for abandoned boys up to the age of eighteen. It happened, there, that my salt loss abated and even ceased for a time.

"After my fifteenth birthday, I started to lose salt again, and required relentless needle sticks to measure the salt in my blood. But in my science class I learned how to measure the salt content in certain substances. And, by tasting my urine and then verifying the exact amount of salt I was losing, I could, within two months, come close to accurately detecting my salt loss by taste alone without verification. There was no need for being stuck after that. Instead, I just tasted my urine and replaced the estimated loss with salt pills. Then all testing stopped; it was assumed I was cured, but I never revealed what I was doing to keep my salt balanced.

"The things I read in scripture gave me the strength to fight on. It was as if the mystical properties of salt had been transferred to my body . . . Shall I continue?"

Have mercy, the Voice whispered.

Rupert stretched and covered a yawn.

"Listen carefully to this." Rupert abruptly got up from where he was sitting and picked up a book. "Philo said, 'Salt acts as a preservative to bodies, ranking second to the life principle. For just as the life principle causes bodies to escape corruption, so does salt, which more than anything else keeps them strong and makes them immortal.'"

Grinning, Rupert looked to his left in the direction of the Voice: "I *repeat*, causes bodies to escape corruption."

After determining the salt content in his urine, Rupert took the equivalent replacement in two cups of bouillon soup and went to sleep.

19

Both Egyptians, and others who are particular about religious observance, use this salt in their sacrifices, as being purer than sea-salt.

~ LUCIUS FLAVIUS ARRIANUS

DEWEY TOOK A BITE of his BLT, then wiped a bit of mayonnaise from the side of his mouth. "Anything on the backgrounds?"

"Nothing," said Luganos, dabbing his sore chin with a Kleenex.

"What about the druggie?"

"Small shit, no relation to the others, no connections."

Dewey rustled in his seat. "Another week gone, and we got nothing." He leaned in. "You know, the Doc said there might be a connection between the victims. I didn't follow his reasoning at the time."

"I don't buy it. Still looks like random killing to me."

"But we got nothing so far."

"So we keep looking. Something will turn up."

Dewey leaned back in his chair. "Suppose the Doc's right—and I'm only guessing now—but say he is. Shouldn't we dig into that? He's a smart guy. If we get another note, we'll need to call him anyway. Let's call him and go over it again."

"You really think he can help?" Luganos began tapping his left foot. Dewey folded his hands. "You don't like him, do you?"

"I wouldn't say that; I wouldn't say that at all."

Luganos squeezed at the fresh pimple on his chin, popping out a bit of clear fluid, which caused Dewey to look away.

∞

Christian was excited to receive Dewey's call. He definitely wanted to stay close to what was happening. It hadn't been long since their first meeting, and they wanted to see him again. In the meantime, he'd met with Father Joseph several times, and all went well. But he knew he had to be careful: Greenberg had warned him about keeping a low profile.

Again, he felt guilt as he realized, somewhat shamefully, that the outlandish method of killing was the primary reason he was eager to stay involved. He had undergone a change; he could feel it: the ease with which his ethics had strayed; agreeing to help the police, principally, to get the story more than to catch a killer. Would he have been as quick to get involved with any other scenario?

His mind drifted back to Jimmy Matzara, his former chief resident and one of his idols. Jimmy was a superb doctor, soft spoken, and a man of great integrity. Christian thought back to a night during his internship when they had worked together as a team. Christian was called to see two patients simultaneously. The first patient was a seventeen-year-old female asthmatic who had taken a turn for the worst. After a thorough examination, he determined the patient was stable. After speaking with the nurses on the floor, he sat to document his findings. A few words into his note, he received an urgent call about the second patient, as of yet unseen. He told the head nurse—one of the most-respected nurses in the hospital—he'd return as soon as he could to finish his note.

Within ten minutes of his leaving the floor, the first patient suffered an acute event, deteriorated, and died. When he returned to the floor, Jimmy was there. Christian explained he had just left the patient minutes before and she had appeared stable at the time, but because of the other urgent call, he could not complete his note. The head nurse verified Christian's words.

Christian said, "I'll complete that note now."

"You shouldn't do that," said Jimmy.

"Why?"

"Because it doesn't truthfully represent what happened. The note was not written before she died. If you fill it in now, it would be after the fact and, at the very least, ethically misleading."

"But I want to indicate my findings when I saw her. The nurses saw me examine her and we all agreed she looked stabled. No one will know if I finish the note now; besides, it would look better in the chart."

"But we would know."

"But Jimmy . . ."

"You didn't do anything wrong. So sign what you've written and write a new note, explaining your findings and how you were called away. That would be the ethical thing to do."

That single incident had a profound effect on Christian. Since that day, whenever he faced a difficult decision, he'd think back to Jimmy and that lesson in ethics. *Would Jimmy approve of his decisions now?* Probably not. But the timing was too perfect. What a great chapter for his book. So, for the present, he'd put aside his guilt, deciding that if, in fact, he helped catch the killer, God and Jimmy would understand.

∞

Luganos met Christian outside Dewey's office with a weak handshake and no smile. The detective wore a black turtleneck, too hot for the time of year. And the dark stubble of a new beard gave him a severe look. Christian noted the infected hair follicles peeking out of the dark whiskers on Luganos's chin. He wanted to advise how to treat them but said nothing.

"We think we're dealing with a serial killer." Dewey was standing by the open window, smoking a cigar as he spoke. "We call them 'serial' when they commit three or more killings in a specific period of time. But we only have two definite deaths. Serial killers are usually White males, age twenty-five to fifty, and middle class. Most of them come from a broken home, where they've either been mistreated or sexually abused. All suffered various forms of rejection, and some even admit that God or the Devil was telling them to do all sorts of things. To date, our murders look like random killings. Two victims had minor rap sheets, but we can't establish a relationship between the two. We still don't have much to go on, and we're looking for any leads. The interviews with relatives and friends didn't help."

Dewey walked back to his chair, sat, leaned back, and nodded at Luganos to continue.

"So far, the victims are two Whites—a male and a female—and one African American man. One Jew, one Catholic, and one Muslim. You suggested the victims might be connected. If true, that would be important." Luganos paused to add emphasis to his following words. "I personally feel the murders are random, and the salt hocus-pocus is just a ploy to confuse us."

If Luganos had intended to offend Christian using the term, "hocus-pocus," he'd succeeded. Christian gave the detective a long look.

"You could be right, but I suggest that, as you put it, this salt 'hocus-pocus' may be more critical than you think. Your readiness to dismiss its importance may reflect your unfamiliarity with salt symbolism."

"What the fuck does that mean?"

Christian's facial expression didn't change. His skill as a teacher had given him lots of experience with aggressive colleagues. That was common in academia, and definitely part of any Black man's life. To be doubted and questioned was nothing new; it was almost expected.

Christian turned to Dewey. "The fact is, salt has been used to kill two, maybe three people, and our killer's quotes are all about salt. The only clues you have at this point are, shall we say, are the salt things."

Luganos began to speak, but Christian politely raised his hands.

"Bear with me, Detective. I'll concede that up to this point, you've not found anything that connects the victims. Does that mean nothing exits?" Christian raised his hands again, as if surrendering—a gesture he meant to be conciliatory. "To me, our killer indicates that his victims, collectively speaking, have all done something wrong. In his note, he used the term, 'these.' I interpret that to mean the victims—plural. Why would the killer pick people at random and speak as if he knew something special about all of them? I admit this is my personal opinion, and I may be wrong, but I assume that's why you called me here: to give my opinion."

"We deal in facts, Doctor." Luganos's voice was clipped.

Christian turned back to Dewey. "The killer also implies the victims have broken a covenant, and that might be crucial."

Luganos leaned forward. "What covenant?"

"I don't know," admitted Christian.

"Doctor, we all break vows or so-called covenants every day. Isn't it possible that your special interests prevent you from seeing anything but a salt-Bible scenario?"

"Hardly," Christian replied softly. "The symbolism of salt is very complicated." *Luganos has no concept of the connection between salt and the covenants.* He continued: "Few people have this in-depth knowledge of salt and the ability to connect it so appropriately to quotes from scripture. The killer may be unbalanced, but he is no fake. He's out to correct some wrong . . ."

"This killer clearly wants to play with us—fake us out," Luganos insisted with a slight raising of his voice.

Christian stood up and flexed his right knee. "For centuries, even before the birth of Christ, and certainly afterward, sprinkling salt was mandatory in certain religious rites and offerings to the Gods.

"If, for argument's sake, we're dealing with some kind of religious or sacrificial rite, then the salt was not left to taunt us. If he's a religious zealot, it may be a necessary part of whatever he's doing. Since we have no evidence that the salt was left as a taunt, it might be wrong to assume so. That's not to say we can't put it to good use."

Luganos exhaled and stared at Christian. "I believe we have a difference of opinion."

"Agreed," said Christian, politely, nodding. "If I'm correct and he's not using the salt as a diversion, we might be able to predict his moves."

"Is that so?" asked Luganos, a smirk across his lips.

"We have an advantage in that we also know something about salt."

Dewey pointed at Christian. "Doctor, we need to give the press something. Do you have an opinion on that, since obviously you think you have a feel for our killer?"

"What do you gain by saying anything?" asked Christian.

"I think he wants recognition, and are we not obligated to warn the public that a killer is on the loose? And at the same time, we might pacify him or her." Luganos had left his chair.

"You were saying, Doc?" Dewey said.

"I agree that the public is at risk, but I wonder what we gain by recognizing him."

"Failure to recognize him may cause him to act again." Luganos was now talking through a tightened jaw.

"Is there a correlation between the number of murders that a serial killer commits and the final apprehension?" asked Christian.

"No, not a strict correlation; but there is a relationship between the number of killings and mistakes that lead to an arrest," responded Dewey. "Why do you ask?"

"It's unlikely he'll stop, no matter what we do. Do you agree?" Christian looked at Luganos, his voice more diplomatic.

"I agree." Luganos's tone was also diplomatic.

"Why acknowledge him at all? If he gets mad or frustrated, he'll make a mistake and give us the chance to get him."

"Doctor, are you suggesting that we allow him to kill again?"

"No, but you must admit that unless something else surfaces, we may have to wait until he makes a mistake."

20

All flesh is dead and part of a lifeless carcass; but the virtue of salt being added to it, like a soul, gives it a pleasing relish and poignancy.

– PLUTARCH

LUGANOS LOOKED into the small hand mirror and examined the two erupted pimples on his chin. He squeezed out a tiny bit of pus, which he removed with a tissue. He lit a cigarette and leaned back in his chair and opened his copy of *Playboy*. His phone rang.

"Luganos here."

"Luganos—my man! My *main* man."

"Jenkins?"

"Yeah, Jenkins. Alive, and looking for the big story. Let's talk about health."

"Health?"

"Ours, my man—yours, and definitely mine."

"What are you talking about?"

"I've heard that folks with high blood pressure and bad tickers hafta watch how much salt they swallow. Are you listening?"

"Look, Jenkins, I'm busy."

"I *said*, are you listening?!"

"I'm listening."

"I just learned that nobody—you hear me?—nobody, should ever get salt *mainlined* 'cause it can fuck you up. You know what I'm saying?"

Luganos's heart skipped a beat. After a long pause, he said, "I'm not following you."

"You know exactly what I'm talking about. Listen up, dog, there's a big story cooking, and I want it. I need it."

When Luganos didn't answer, Jenkins continued. "Looka here, my contacts filled me in. I know all about it! I need the facts to break it right, do it some justice."

"I can't say anything about it. That's straight from the boss."

"Fuck Dewey! I never liked that pig. I need this, man. You owe me, and you know it. I hear a lot of shit in the street, and I been good to you. You know what I'm saying?"

A long pause followed.

"Hold tight, give me a little time, and maybe we can deal." Luganos sat forward in his chair, knowing this was trouble. Jenkins was a low life, a bottom-feeder, the worst type of crime reporter, but he was a good contact for what happened in the street. He'd fed Luganos crucial information many times over.

"Look, man, I'm not fucking around. If you don't give me something, I'll go with what I got."

"I'll call you later." Luganos left his desk, went to the water cooler, and took two Tylenol and his acid-killing pill.

∞

At five-thirty that afternoon, Luganos and Jenkins sat opposite each other at a café on Bleeker Street. Jenkins—tall, honey-brown, with a thin, pointed face—sat with a toothpick in his mouth. He made an unsavory sucking sound as he drew saliva through a decaying tooth he'd been picking at. He swallowed the debris from the cavity, then placed a fresh toothpick in his mouth.

"Okay, whatcha got?"

"You tell me what you know." Luganos decided to be careful, knowing he was at a slight disadvantage.

"Shit, two dead people, killed with salt, mainlined. No signs of violence. That's all I got."

Luganos lit a cigarette, pausing to think of the right response and how to slow things down. He found Jenkins truly offensive, especially his breath, which was a mixture of stale coffee, cigarettes, and decay. He fixated on the dark, irregular moles on Jenkins's face.

"There's not much more to tell. Dewey's called in a consultant, a doctor from Mercy, some kind of expert, to figure things out." Luganos paused.

"And? Keep going! What does he think?"

Luganos hesitated to give the impression that he was divulging privileged information, which, in fact, he was.

"The Doctor thinks the killer is a nut job, maybe a lunatic, freaked out about mystical shit about salt, like it was alive and had power. I think it's all bullshit; killing and then leaving salt at the scene. Probably some smart ass, maybe a psycho, but someone smooth enough to make it look like a spooky movie. This killer is playing with us."

"Think the expert would talk to me?"

"Hell, no! Officially, nothing has been given to the press because Dewey wants it that way."

"Does anyone else know about this doctor expert?"

"No. And keep it that way."

"Is the doc a shrink?"

"No, he's some kind of kidney doctor, supposed to know a lot about salt—all the spooky shit. And, oh yes, he's what you call a 'brother.'"

"A brother? Black? No shit!" Jenkins took another sip of his coffee, unwrapped a new toothpick, and placed it in his mouth processing this last revelation. "What do you mean 'freaked out about salt'?"

Jenkins continued to pick at the decayed tooth on the side of his mouth. Luganos looked away.

"There's supposed to be voodoo stuff wrapped up in salt. The Doc thinks all that shit got to the killer and fried his brain."

"Why is he killing people?"

"I don't know."

"Give me his name."

Luganos hesitated again, which only served to excite Jenkins even more.

"I'm not going to call the fuck, okay?"

"It's Dr. Christian; Malcolm Christian."

21

*Salt is white and pure—there must
be something holy in salt.*

- NATHANIEL HAWTHORNE

BRICE FELT THE DISCOMFORT AGAIN: a tightness in the center of his chest radiating down his left arm and up to the angle of his jaw. He paused, pressed his chest, and belched.

Relief. *I'm paying the price for my breakfast; bacon and eggs with peppers can be deadly.* He didn't want to think of the alternative: his heart. Eight months ago, Brice had angioplasty for a blocked vessel on the side of his heart. That was when the symptoms began with tightness similar to what he was now feeling. His doctor told him if the chest pain lasted less than a minute, it probably wasn't his heart. Today, the pain had lasted less than thirty seconds on each occasion.

He'd spent most of the morning listening to Rosalyn Tureck's handling of Bach's *Well-Tempered Clavier*. At 10 a.m., he picked up the *Daily* from outside his door. What he read in the crime section made him hurry to the phone and dial Christian.

"Christian, have you seen the *Daily*? It's on page two of the crime section."

"What's on page two?"

"The murders."

"What? What does it say?"

"'Killer loose in NYC.' It goes on to say, 'The killer is most likely a psycho, according to Dr. Malcolm Christian, chief of the kidney section at Mercy Hospital, who's been called in as a consultant on the case.' It's right here, Christian."

"Holy shit. Greenberg is going to go nuts. Thanks." Christian hung up the phone. *Dewey said nothing would be given to the press. And I never said the killer was a psycho.*

∞

"Who the fuck is responsible for this?" Dewey added another pack of NutraSweet to his black coffee.

Luganos looked up, feigning puzzlement. "I don't know, but the mention of several murders makes me think it's the coroner's office. I'm sure it wasn't Giles, though."

"This is bad," Dewey said, putting a Nicorette in his mouth. "I don't want to spook him. He may change his pattern, might even think we're on his tail."

"We're not on his tail," said Luganos.

"I know that, but we're waiting for him to slip."

"Remember, I wanted to give the press something before this shit."

"I don't like the coverage. The Doc never called the guy a psycho—at least not in the way the article says." Dewey slammed the edition of the *Daily* on his desk.

"I agree," said Luganos. "This guy's is toying with us; he's very sane, but what now?"

Dewey sat down. "We've already received a lot of calls, so I've prepared a brief statement. It's unfortunate the doc's name was mentioned."

"Do you think he minds?" Luganos leaned back and rubbed his chin.

"What do you mean?" asked Dewey.

"The Doc strikes me as something of a dandy. He's giving lectures and writing a book about salt. It'll probably be good press."

Dewey looked at Luganos for a long second. "Do you think he leaked it?"

Luganos took his time to answer. He rubbed his chin and narrowed his eyes. "I didn't mean to give that impression."

22

The French people employ the word "salt" metaphorically . . . thus, in speaking of the lack of piquancy or pointedness in a dull sermon or address, they say, "There was no salt in that discourse." And of a brilliant, favorite writer, they remark, "He has sprinkled his writing with salt by handfuls."

~ ROBERT MEANS LAWRENCE, MD

CHRISTIAN STOOD JUST OUTSIDE Greenberg's office, looking at the paneled wall of mounted pictures. Among the photos, one showed Christian, Forsyth, and Greenberg standing together at the opening of the ICU twenty years ago. Another showed two nuns in spotless white habits demonstrating the transfer of a patient from gurney to bed. These pictures stirred feelings of a magical time in his life when the nuns played a major role in the hospital; a time passed and a time he missed.

Greenberg's office was in disarray: papers, folders, and schedules everywhere. He looked up at Christian as he entered. "Well, Sherlock, what's all this shit about?"

"What shit?"

"The stuff in the *Daily*. You and the police?" Greenberg's face was intense, his head to the side, his eyes narrowed.

"They reached out to me."

"About what?"

"That's confidential."

Greenberg raised his hands in a gesture of surrender. "We need to stay under the radar until this thing is settled and the Good Father is *outta* here. He's not happy about seeing your name and the hospital's name in the *Daily* and your referring to someone as a 'psycho.' He's a psychologist and didn't think the noun was appropriate."

"Did he say that?"

"Is the Pope Catholic?"

"I never spoke to the press and never used that word."

"We don't want to piss him off." Greenberg leaned forward. "The article said you'd be helping with an ongoing investigation. Is that true?"

"I don't know, and I can't discuss it."

"If there's any bad press—anything attached to your name or the hospital's name"—Greenberg leaned back, making his point—"he may ask you to let it go."

"Well, if he does, I'll politely tell him, 'I don't think so.'"

Greenberg looked away at the open window and drummed the fingers of his right hand. "Christian, you're not thinking straight. Don't mess this up."

"Alf, he may be a father, but he's not *my* father."

"I understand that, but we're in a bind. How many times have you met?"

"Three or four times; all business, but—get this—he wanted to know how tough it was being a minority in the good ol' days."

"What? You're kiddin' me."

"You heard me. The same routine: surprised and absolutely impressed at my achievements."

Greenberg looked down at his desk and shuffled a pile of disorganized papers. "Keep the name of the institution out of the headlines."

Christian went to leave but hesitated at the door. "For your information, I don't think the authorities like my input."

"Good."

Christian gave a perfunctory salute and left the office without saying another word.

∞

That evening, Rupert sat at the small white Formica table, its surface chipped and the black undercoating showing. He sipped a cup of tea. Under a dull light from a single overhead bulb, he studied the Bible and tried to ignore the babble of the Voice, which craved his attention. It was dark outside, and the occasional buzz of an electric insect killer marked the tragic ending of whatever was drawn to the light outside his kitchen window.

Why did you choose salt? The Voice was deferential.

"It's rather simple. In Genesis, God gave man a body and a soul and expected him to cherish both. In Romans 6:12, He warned us not to let sin reign within our mortal body. All of them let sin into their bodies."

That's why you chose salt? The Voice was whispering, pressing Rupert to elaborate.

Rupert whispered in return. "Salt is sacred. Didn't God choose salt to seal his covenant with Aaron, with David, and with Moses? You remember."

Rupert took a sip of the dark Darjeeling tea, especially chosen for its effectiveness in soothing bladder pain. He'd felt weak, weaker than the day before, a drained sensation, and, this morning, he'd found a large amount of salt in his urine. He read aloud an excerpt from The Wisdom of Sirach:

> "His blessing covers the land like a river and saturates the dry land like a flood. As he turns water into saltwater, so the hea-

then will experience his wrath . . . From the beginning good things have been created for the good, just as evils have been created for the sinners. The elements necessary for man's life are water, fire, iron, and salt . . . All these things prove good to the godly just as they turn into evil for the sinful."

He closed the book and picked up the *Daily* and read the story for the third time. His face burned, and his scalp tightened.

The Voice hissed: *Psycho! My, my, I thought dear Dr. Christian was more refined than that.* Then the Voice laughed, mockingly.

"Shut up!"

Rupert stood up abruptly and felt dizzy. This wooziness always happened whenever he moved too quickly, or when his salt was low, or both. The doctor called it "Orthostasis." *What an elegant word for such a dreadful feeling.* He walked slowly to his bed and reclined.

The Voice, alive again, continued: *He thinks you're shit. The word "psycho" is so demeaning. You have helped all of them redeem themselves! The corruptible worm corrupts all things and there is nothing on earth neither wood, nor earth nor flesh, which it does not consume, save salt.*

23

*Salt is not found in witches' kitchens,
nor at a devils' feast.*

~ THE BROTHERS GRIMM

RUPERT STOOD IN LINE at the supermarket on Sixth Avenue and watched the clerk—slow-moving and eating a bag of potato chips—drag items over a screechy scanner.

A stocky pale-White man was standing directly in front of Rupert, talking to a friend. He'd noticed the pair earlier, when they'd opened a carton of candy bars and slipped several into their pockets. Rupert saw them again when they cut in line directly in front of him. He said nothing.

The stocky man had a shaved head and a blue ship's anchor tattooed on his neck. "Yeah, I fooled those fuckers," he was saying. "The good old U.S. Navy and the New York City Fire Department—and got a pension from *boft* of them."

"Shit, Arnie, how you do that?" his friend asked, bringing a hand to his mouth to cover his laughter.

The two smelled of weed, and Arnie popped several pills straight from a small prescription bottle. "Yeah, man, I faked seasickness using some shit called 'cordite.' That stuff can make you puke all day long. All you gotta do is chew and swallow the juice." Arnie took a candy bar from his coat jacket and stuffed it into his mouth. "Can you imagine a sailor who gets seasick? They made me get X-rays of my head and neck. And they found an *incidental* bone defect in my neck, man."

"A what?" asked his friend.

"An incidental bone defect—something they didn't expect to find that looks suspicious. And they couldn't tell how long I had it, or what caused it. I didn't know nothing about it, because it never caused any pain. They kept on asking didn't it hurt, moving my neck around like it was supposed to hurt. Shit, I began thinking maybe it should hurt. In the meantime, my discharge came through. Since it took three months before I could leave the navy, I got myself assigned to the medical clinic as a clerk. I destroyed my X-rays showing my defect along with the report and replaced them with a normal set of rays and a normal report."

"Why, man?" Arnie's friend's eyelids had begun to droop.

"I read something in a book that gave me an idea. This was my meal ticket."

As Rupert listened, the Voice began screaming, *Damn it!*

"When I got out, I qualified for the FDNY. In fact, I moved to the top of the list using my points as a veteran." Arnie took another big bite of the candy bar.

Ain't that a bitch! screamed the Voice.

"Now, here's the good part: after a year, I was assigned to Engine Seventeen in Harlem, and during an alarm, I faked a fall and said I hurt my neck. X-rays were taken, and guess what? They saw that shit in my neck, that little ol' incidental bony defect.

"I told them I never had a problem before I fell. And I told them the navy took some X-rays of my head and neck at one time. They got those reports, and they were normal. So, the fall musta' caused the defect, right? And this time, I said it hurt like a mother. I complained for eight months about pain, went on sick leave, did rehab, but refused surgery and finally got out with a pension because of that incidental bony defect."

As Rupert listened, the Voice pleaded with him to do something. It screamed over and over until Rupert became dizzy and had to leave the checkout line. He walked to the rear of the store where trash was stacked and vomited into a cardboard box filled with rotting fruit. When he returned to the line, the pair was gone.

Rupert left the store and walked downtown along Sixth Avenue in the direction of the World Trade Center. The Voice had quieted to a constant whisper of vulgarities. He entered Bigalow's Pharmacy and went directly to the checkout clerk to request an item. On the counter he noticed a number of prescriptions. Suddenly, Rupert received a harsh bump from behind. When he turned, he saw Arnie's pale face.

"I was in line but had to leave for just a second—do you mind?"

Rupert, off balance, recovered quickly enough to say, "No, not at all."

Arnie, in front of Rupert again, proceeded to count his prescriptions, one by one, calling out each by name. The clerk returned and placed a package of Egyptian purified salt tablets on the counter.

"Are these mine?" asked Arnie.

"No" said the clerk. "They belong to this gentleman." Arnie turned and looked at Rupert.

"You take them, too?" asked Arnie.

"Yes." Rupert felt his jaw tighten.

Arnie reached into his pocket and pulled out a candy bar and took three quarters of the bar in one bite. Rupert felt his stomach churn, and saliva filled his mouth the way it did just before he vomited.

"Do you work out?" Arnie, eyes red and glassy, was making conversation.

"No."

Arnie wore a tight-fitting shirt that displayed his buff physique. Arnie pointed in the direction of the salt tablets and said, "I take the stuff by the bucket because I sweat so much."

"One must be careful: salt can be a friend, but it can also be a foe." He smiled.

"How so?"

"Oh, it's a long story."

Arnie frowned, concerned by the warning, as Rupert knew he would be. Rupert could easily spot the health freaks who did trendy things to build attractive bodies—while at the same time smoking and drinking and filling their lives with sin. *They've forgotten God's gift to them,* the Voice hissed.

Arnie checked out at counter and walked in the direction of the exit. Rupert paid for items and headed for the exit. Rupert saw Arnie standing at the exit alone.

"Can this shit hurt ya?" Arnie pressed the question as he opened the door and politely motioned Rupert to leave first.

"Yes, if you have high blood pressure or a failing heart, for example, too much salt can be dangerous." Rupert paused and then tapped Arnie's chest twice, just above his heart. "And there are other ways that salt can harm if your soul is not clean."

Rupert saw the puzzled look on Arnie's face.

Today was judgment day for Arnie. All the things he'd done—the double pensions, everything—would be redeemed. Deformed Rupert, the ill-born, self-appointed messenger of God, was alive and working.

"I would be happy to give you some reading material. It's one of my favorite topics." Rupert bumped Arnie's shoulder in a buddy fashion. "Jot your number down for me; I'll definitely call you soon—very soon."

After leaving Arnie, Rupert walked back to his apartment enjoying the late evening sky as it changed colors: a yellow, transforming into a deep, fiery red-orange as the light faded. The Voice, now absolutely pacified, chose the words of Saint Marcarius to describe Arnie: *And for his momentary pleasures, he will not obtain the incorruptible pleasure desired by his soul, but having become insipid salt, he is more miserable than all of me.*

24

*During the nights let the fields turn white,
let the broad plain bring forth salt crystals,
let her bosom revolt, that no plant
come forth, no grain sprout.*

– ATRASHASIS OF BABYLON

THE DEAD MAN LAY ON HIS BACK wearing a damp discolored T-shirt; a note was placed next to him on the couch. The apartment was clean, with a modern couch and chairs of white vinyl and chrome. An area devoted to free weights and a StairMaster occupied a space near a bright window.

Luganos stooped to his knees to look at the floor around the couch. "No salt," he said, sweeping his hand across the floor and under the couch.

"Nowhere," agreed Giles. "Just the note and the needle puncture."

Luganos gently passed a gloved hand over the dead man's shirt. "His shirt is wet."

"He was soaked when we got here. He must have been doused after he was lying down." Giles disguised a half-yawn as he lit a cigarette.

"How do you know it was after he was lying down?" Luganos asked.

"I found a pool of fluid in the suprasternal notch." Giles pointed to the hollow area directly below Arnie's Adam's apple. "And wet spots on the couch behind his neck. The note looks like it was also splashed. Maybe water. We're taking a sample for analysis."

"What do you think it means?"

"I don't know. Maybe he vomited up some fluid as he died, although it doesn't look like vomitus or saliva." Giles went into his bag and opened a brown envelope, producing a small vial. "This is it." The fluid was slightly opaque but contained no particles.

"Do you have enough for analysis?"

"Plenty. We'll do everything."

Luganos turned to Dewey, who had just arrived.

"No salt." A smile crept across Luganos's face. "How do you think the Doc will explain this?"

∞

Christian arrived at Dewey's office an hour after being called. He was brought to a conference room with metal chairs and a metal folding table. Dewey was looking out of a window, and Luganos sat examining his notebook. A bulky overhead projector was set up for viewing.

"We think it's him, but no trace of salt this time," Luganos said as soon as Christian walked in. He had a whimsical smile on his face.

"You said he left a note?" Christian asked.

Dewey switched on the projector and displayed the note. Christian read the words out loud:

> ". . . Take from them all blindness of heart. Free them from all the snares of Satan by which they have been held. Open to them, Lord, the gate of your mercy. Then, impregnated by the symbol of your wisdom, may they be relieved of the corruption of all evil desires . . ."

Luganos spoke first: "Do you think it's him?"

Dewey sat forward and looked at Christian intently. "I want to be certain we're dealing with the same bird, not a copycat."

"I think it's him. This quotation has the same flavor as the other note."

"Are you familiar with the quotation?" There was a hint of sarcasm in Luganos's question.

"I'm not sure." Still staring at the screen, Christian felt Luganos's gaze and heard a quiet sigh.

"He doesn't mention salt in the note, and we didn't find salt at the scene." Luganos tilted his head to the side. "Have things changed, Doc?" His smirk had returned. "Maybe our friend is changing his tactics, switching from your salt business to something new? Maybe a different touch, another way of playing with us?"

Christian sat back and gave Luganos a long look. "You're correct; he doesn't use the word, 'salt,' but he says, 'the symbol of wisdom.' That's a phrase often used to refer to salt in religious writings. More importantly, the note leads me back to the conclusion that the victims, collectively, have done something wrong, and our man is going to fix it with salt."

"But where's the salt, Professor?"

Christian smiled, sensing the man's eagerness to put him on the spot. "More than likely in the victim's blood. I assume that's being tested for?"

"As we speak."

"Then we should know very soon, shouldn't we?"

"Why do you think he's changed his usual MO, if in fact, it's our guy?" asked Dewey.

"You mean no visible salt? I'm not certain." Christian narrowed his eyes. "Tell me about the crime scene."

Luganos sighed, then described what they'd discovered.

When Luganos finished, Dewey said, "I would feel much better if he'd left a little salt."

"But I believe he did," said Christian.

The smile drained from Lugano's face, and he looked at Dewey. "Where?"

As Christian was about to answer Luganos, his phone rang.

"This is Christian . . . When? Is he stable?"

Luganos glanced at Dewey, a peeved look on his face. He rustled in his chair.

Christian folded his cell phone and looked at Dewey. "Brice had a heart attack. I should see him. I'll get back as soon as I can."

Luganos stood abruptly. "You were about to tell us about the missing salt." His hands opened as if he were expecting an answer.

Christian stepped to the side. "This can wait; I said I'll be back as soon as I can."

"The test results are expected about three," said Dewey.

"Good," Christian said and began to leave.

"Let us know what's up when you get there, Doc," said Dewey.

∞

In the taxi, Christian reviewed the note in his head. He knew it was the killer, without a doubt. *This guy is smarter than I thought. He knows his Bible and his physiology.*

Christian could still hear Luganos saying, "Where's the salt?" He smiled to himself, knowing the answer was in the wet T-shirt.

∞

Christian entered the busy emergency room and met the medical resident he'd spoken to on the phone. He was directed to station four.

The hospital bed seemed too small for Brice's large frame. The ill-fitting hospital gown was rumpled and looked uncomfortable. Brice still had his socks on. An oxygen monitor was attached to one finger, and his broad chest was covered in EKG monitor leads. An IV bag hung above the bed with a slow drip of fluid flowing into his left arm.

"Well, well, what do we have here?" Christian noted the EKG configuration showing the acute cardiac damage.

"Not a good day, my friend," said Brice.

"How do you feel?"

"Fine, considering. They gave me something for the pain, and now I'm just a little woozy. I didn't take my medicine for a few days because I felt nauseated. I didn't call because I was afraid you might put me in the hospital. I certainly didn't want that."

Christian knew that Brice was deathly frightened of hospitals.

"When will I go upstairs?"

"Soon, I hope. For now, things look good. Your pulse and blood pressure are stable, but you do have some damage. Better rest, and I'll check back after you get settled."

∞

At the other end of the emergency room, a group of nursing students were being quizzed. When the session ended, the supervising nurse walked to the patient chart rack. Rupert loved covering the emergency room, even on short notice like today, when the regular charge nurse called in sick. He turned to the resident and asked, "Is this a patient of Dr. Christian's?"

"Yes. I think he's a close friend, and he's going to the CCU from here."

"Ah, in that case, we must do all we can to make him feel at home."

∞

By 3 p.m., Christian was back in Dewey's office.

"How is Brice doing?" Dewey's asked.

"He's definitely had a heart attack, but things are stable. He's in the coronary unit at Mercy."

"Will he be okay?"

"I hope so."

"Can we pick up where we left off," said Dewey, pointing to Luganos.

"The sodium chloride concentration in the blood was lethal. The brain and other tissues showed severe damage caused by the salt. The fluid collected from below the Adam's apple was …

"Urine," Christian interjected.

Luganos looked up from the paper and whispered, "Precisely."

Dewey, a disgusted look on his face, whispered, "You mean that fucker pissed on the victim?"

"Precisely," Luganos said again.

"What do you make of that?" Dewey looked at Christian.

Before Christian could respond, Luganos jumped in. "Pretty kinky, don't you think?"

Christian waited a few seconds before responding. "No, not kinky. It was his way of leaving salt."

Luganos clasped his hands together, as if beginning to pray, and widened his eyes. "Are you telling us that pissing on the dead guy has some symbolic significance? It looks to me like he's continuing to fuck with us, Doc."

"No," said Christian, shaking his head. "You may think he's vulgar, but this isn't about insults; it's more than that."

"*What?*" yelled Dewey. "I'd like to wring his fucking neck!"

"Let me explain. In past centuries, according to myth, urine and health were linked. Even today, some Native Americans still give small quantities of urine to their infants at birth. Why? Urine contains salt. It has to do with salt as a purifier. All the body fluids, especially urine, contain significant amounts of salt under normal circumstances. In fact, we excrete the salt the body doesn't need directly in our urine. And over centuries, it was assumed that the magical and symbolic power of salt was transferred to urine because of its significant salt content. For all intents and purposes, urine became a substitute for salt, at least, metaphorically. So, in fact, he *did* leave salt, but in the form of his urine."

Christian looked directly at Luganos before continuing. "He's not kinky, and he didn't change his MO. He simply slipped into the past and drew from the unique history of salt."

The room was silent. Christian knew he had delivered a solid blow; he could feel Lugano's discomfort.

As a seasoned teacher, he waited a moment longer, then broke the silence in a low voice. "This is our man. And he's pretty smart."

25

*The soul is the salt of the body; faith the salt
of the soul by which it is preserved.*

~ EPHRAIM THE SYRIAN

BRICE'S LOWER BACK ACHED from the rigid gurney, and the morphine had made him thirsty. The intravenous line in his left arm burned, and his bladder was distended. A full hour had passed since Christian left, and he was still in the emergency room. He rang the buzzer for the nurse.

When the nurse arrived, she peeked behind the curtain.

"How long before I can go upstairs?" he asked.

The nurse flashed a practiced smile. "Things are really busy, and the beds are being moved as fast as possible."

Before he could respond, she was gone. Then Brice noticed that the musical popping of the cardiac monitor, absolutely regular up to this point, now changed its rhythm. He closed his eyes and tried to relax, but the pain in his bladder was intense. Because of the way he was hooked up to the monitor, the nurse would have to help him place his penis in the urinal. He didn't want that. He decided to wait a while longer.

His chest pain started again. Brice rang the buzzer.

"I'm getting chest pains." The nurse took his pulse and watched the monitor for a full minute, counting the irregular beats. She then adjusted a dial to deliver more oxygen. "I'll give you a little more morphine and see if that helps." After the injection, his chest pain eased, but as the pain receded, his vision blurred. Then his cubicle took on an elongated shape. Suddenly, a nurse's aide pulled back the curtain to refill his water pitcher. Her features were distorted—her face resembled that of a donkey. He began to sweat. He rang the buzzer again.

"Call the supervisor of this fucking place!" He pointed directly at the nurse as she opened the curtain.

"Mr. Brice, we'll move you as soon as there's a bed available."

"Call the supervisor!" A light sheen of sweat covered his brown skin. Even though he felt strange and dopey, he was shocked to hear these coarse words coming from his own lips.

"I'll call the supervisor right away, Mr. Brice."

∞

"My name is Rupert Pike. May I help you?"

Brice was scratching at his sheets. His eyes were wide, and his tongue was licking his upper lip. "When am I going to be treated like a human being? I want to get out of this place before I get hurt!"

"Mr. Brice, we're trying to get you upstairs; please refrain from using profanity." Rupert's tone was clipped.

Brice lifted himself on his elbows and glared at Rupert, his teeth clenched. "Get away from me." Rupert closed the curtain, went directly to the nursing station, and wrote a note documenting Brice's profanity. He then called upstairs.

∞

Twenty minutes later, Brice was transferred to the coronary care unit. The new bed was uncomfortable, and amid the sounds of respirators, beeps, buzzers, and the swift movements of the nurses, his anxiety increased.

At the foot of his bed, a nurse spoke quietly to the resident in charge of his case.

Brice sat up abruptly. "What's going on here?"

"We're trying to get you settled in, Mr. Brice," the nurse said.

"Get away from me."

Aware of the problem in the emergency room, the nurse immediately placed calls to Rupert, the cardiologist who'd seen Brice earlier, and to Christian.

When Rupert arrived on the floor and was told of Brice's behavior, he personally placed a page to Dr. Christian. Rupert and the nurse then entered Brice's room. When Brice looked up and saw them, he pointed to Rupert.

"You again! I told you to stay away from me!" Brice was now drenched in sweat.

"Mr. Brice, I'm the administrator for this floor. Can I help you?"

"You certainly can. I want to make a formal complaint about the shitty care I'm getting here."

"Mr. Brice, you've just had a heart attack," said the nurse in a kind, sympathetic tone. "Please try to calm down."

"Did you hear me? I want to make a complaint!"

"I'll let Miss Rodriguez take the complaint," Rupert announced. "I doubt that I can continue this conversation any longer." Then he walked away.

Minutes after Rupert left, Christian arrived. He entered the room and found Brice half sitting up, resting on his elbows, his eyes staring upward at the ceiling. Christian immediately knew Brice was not aware of his surroundings. He looked at the overhead monitor: the pulse was up, but the blood pressure was normal. Brice was drenched in sweat. Christian gently pushed Brice back into a lying position and listened to his heart. Next, he examined Brice's pupils. They were severely constricted, pinpoints to be exact. He palpated the four quadrants of the abdomen. The bladder was distended and tender.

Christian considered the situation: an elderly man with a fresh coronary and an abrupt change in mental status. What could explain this sudden change? The possibilities were: an extension of the original cardiac injury, a stroke, a blood clot to the lung, or a drug reaction. With little change in blood pressure and no change in the EKG, a worsening of the heart attack seemed unlikely.

Christian did a quick neurologic examination. The strength and movement in all limbs were normal, and that, for the present, ruled out stroke. The oxygen saturation was normal, and the lung sounds were clear, making a blood clot to the lung less likely. Brice's temperature was normal, so infection was also unlikely. The last possibility, and the one thing that Christian had suspected from the start, was an adverse drug reaction. This condition, commonly seen in elderly patients and often misdiagnosed, presents as a spontaneous, bizarre change in mental status after receiving certain drugs—commonly opiates, like morphine. Christian needed to check the medication list.

As he stepped from Brice's room, he came face-to-face with Rupert. Both men stopped at the door, and without hesitation Rupert spoke: "Mr. Brice wishes to file a complaint."

"A complaint?" Christian held up both hands. "Whoa, wait a minute. He's in no condition to do anything of the kind. Mr. Brice has just had a sudden change in mental status, and I'm trying to find out why."

"Oh, his mental status has been consistently quite nasty," said Rupert.

Christian, disregarding the remark, noted Rupert's title from his identification badge. He'd seen Rupert around the hospital and at large faculty meetings; however, he'd never spoken to him or been formally introduced.

"Mr. Brice is not himself; something new has happened."

Rupert looked over Christian's shoulder at Brice, now wide-eyed and mumbling to himself.

Christian turned to the nurse. "Can I see his medication sheet? I think this is a drug reaction."

"The only meds he's received are aspirin, a beta-blocker, and several doses of morphine sulfate."

"The morphine could do it. His pupils are constricted, and his bladder is distended. These are common side effects of morphine."

"What do I do with this?" Rupert was holding up the patient complaint form. "I can't ignore the complaint; that's against hospital policy and state regulations."

"What's the nature of the complaint?"

Rupert took a long, exaggerated breath and then began: "Thirty minutes ago, I was called to see Mr. Brice in the ER. I'm the acting administrator for both units today. When I spoke to him and tried to explain the delay in getting a bed, he became rude, verbally abusive, and outright profane. I tried to reason with him, but he became more agitated."

"Mr. Pike, I understand your concern, but as his longtime friend, I feel qualified to ask you to disregard the complaint."

Rupert's face remained rigid. He turned to the nurse. "Ms. Rodriguez, I'll leave this complaint form in the chart in case Mr. Brice still wishes to file a complaint. I'll make my own report for quality-assurance purposes." Without looking at Christian, Rupert abruptly turned and left the floor.

Christian watched as Rupert walked to the stairwell and disappeared. He turned to the nurse and ordered a specific drug that would counteract the effects of morphine. Christian directed the resident to pass a catheter and relieve Brice's distended bladder. The diagnosis of adverse drug reaction and acute change in mental status was entered into the chart, and an "Allergy to Opiates" sticker was placed on the front of Brice's chart.

As Christian sat in the nurse's section finishing his note, he replayed his encounter with Rupert. The administrator's peeved demeanor wasn't unusual, constantly having to always deal with bullshit. But there was something else: the gaunt appearance of the man, who looked chronically ill. The man was sick.

Two other things caught Christian's attention. The dark, reddened rash over the back of Rupert's hands, and the odor of Rupert's breath. In clinical medicine, there were two distinct pathologic breath odors—fetors, as they were called: the sweet, fruity smell of exhaled *acetone* by the sick diabetic, and the urine-like odor expelled by patients with kidney failure—*the uremic fetor*. Seasoned clinicians knew them well. But the uremic fetor was seldom encountered these days because treatment for kidney failure was usually instituted before patients reached that stage.

Although Christian's encounter with Rupert had been brief, he was certain he'd detected this unmistakable clinical sign. It wouldn't be the first time Christian met someone working alongside doctors—on a daily basis—who was literally dying.

Christian wondered, briefly, if he should get involved. He'd seen the rash. It looked to be kidney-related, and more importantly, the man's breath was unmistakably diagnostic. He felt ethically obligated to do something, at least be certain the man was evaluated.

He reflected back to his days as an intern. It was a time when the nuns were still in charge of the house staff quarters. Sister Catherine-Claude had cared for Christian's quarters. Diminutive, soft-spoken, and kind, she was born in Ireland and had the most expressive eyes he'd ever seen. They immediately became buddies. One night she told him a patient confided in her that the "Black doctor" told her he also was born out of wedlock and that she shouldn't be ashamed of her beautiful baby son.

After a time, Sister Catherine-Claude told him that she had a heart condition, but all was fine. Several months into their friendship, he noticed that her breathing was labored, and her ankles had begun to swell. He questioned Sister Catherine about her care and about her medicines, but she waved him off, saying it was just her heart, and she was in God's hands. He respectfully backed off, but he privately worried that her recent turn for the worse was not due to her heart condition.

Then, suddenly, Sister Catherine was absent from clinic, and a new nun was assigned to cover her duties. When Christian went to see the superior nun, he was told that Sister Catherine had been admitted to a hospital while on a weekend trip and had died the night before—not from heart disease but from undiagnosed abdominal cancer. Ironically, the kind sister worked in a hospital, around doctors and nurses, and her downhill slide had been missed. Christian vowed he would never let something like that happen again.

He made a mental note to call Dr. Chang, the personnel health director, and ask a few questions about Rupert Pike.

∞

At ten-thirty that evening, Christian visited Brice. The effects of the morphine had been reversed, and he was sleeping peacefully. Christian admired the hospital at night. The quiet wards with their subdued lighting; the nursing stations, calm but busy; and the nuns visiting the sick, their habits gently rustling as they moved about from bed to bed.

Christian listened to his last message: "This is Dewey. Doc, could we meet for a few minutes around nine, tomorrow morning, if possible? The coroner thinks you should review one of the reports."

26

Let your speech always be gracious,
seasoned with salt, so that you may know
how you ought to answer each person.

~ COLOSSIANS 4:6

AT SEVEN-THIRTY THE NEXT MORNING, Christian visited Brice and found him alert and smiling. He handed him the latest edition of *Gramophone*. "You look better this morning."

"Yesterday is foggy; must have been those medications they gave me. I had a nightmare but can't remember what it was about."

"You had a reaction to the morphine, and you acted up. You even wanted to file a complaint."

"Are you serious? You see what hospitals do to me?"

"You went wild in the ER, and I suspect you'll get a visit from some administrator about your complaint; you may have to sign a statement yourself. Get some rest. I'll see you later."

∞

At the Sixth Precinct, Christian was ushered into a conference room. Dewey was standing, and Luganos was sitting at a table, his notebook open in front of him.

"The coroner wants you to see these results," Luganos said, opening to a page in his notebook. "The analysis of the small amount of urine from the suprasternal notch contained this amount of sodium chloride."

"What?" Christian looked at Luganos in disbelief.

"That's what it says. They repeated the analysis three times." Luganos handed his book to Christian.

"That's too much salt in so small a quantity of urine."

"What do you mean?" Dewey interjected.

"The salt we excrete in the urine depends on the amount we consume. A normal person would never excrete that large amount of salt. It's too much in that small sample of urine." Christian sat down and narrowed his eyes. "No salt was found at the scene, and I don't know of any medicine that could produce this load of salt in that small a specimen . . ." Christian's eyes widened as his pulse quickened. "Of course! He's sick! He has kidney disease. He's a salt loser!"

"A salt loser—what the fuck is that?" said Dewey, hunching forward over his desk.

"That would explain these results and, I believe, a number of other things."

At that moment, a clerk entered the room and handed Dewey a piece of paper. Dewey looked at it, then handed it to Christian. It was a report from the coroner's office.

"Yes, yes," Christian muttered, examining the paper. "Now things are clear." He placed the report down on Dewey's desk. "He's definitely suffering from kidney disease."

"How do you know?"

"Not only is the level of salt in his urine too high, but more importantly, there's too little waste in the urine—too small an amount of urea. Urea is one of the major waste products that urine carries out of the body. If your kidneys are functioning, there should be a large amount of urea in the urine. If not, the urea builds up in our blood. That happens when the kidneys are not working. Our man's kidneys cannot retain salt, and they can't excrete his waste products. He's 'uremic'— too much urea, or urine, in his blood."

"Uremic," Dewey said, then repeated in a whisper, mostly to himself: "Too much urine in the blood."

"By leaving us a sample of his urine, he's left us a fingerprint—a clue. We have a start."

Luganos looked at Dewey, then at Christian. Then he stood up, a smile on his Grecian face. He took two paces closer to Christian, opened his arms as if to hug him, and said, "I am impressed, professor."

Christian smiled back and extended his hand to Luganos. They shook.

Dewey walked closer to both of them and placed his hands on theirs and said, "Good, now let's get this fucker."

When their meeting was over, Luganos went back to his office and took two of his acid-killing pills and a Tylenol. His stomach was on fire, and his head throbbed. He thought to himself, *That smart-ass prick.*

27

*It is a grand thing to rise in the world.
The ambition to do so is the very salt of
the earth. It is the parent of all enterprise,
and the cause of all improvement.*

~ ANTHONY TROLLOPE

CHRISTIAN ENJOYED THE WALK up Sixth Avenue to Twelfth Street and the entrance to The New School. His talk began at six-thirty, so he still had a few minutes to spare. The sun was just fading in a still blue sky, and he stood at the front of the building enjoying the pleasant breeze as evening approached.

He entered the building, identified himself, and walked into the auditorium. The place was filled and buzzing. After being introduced, he took the podium, and without saying a word, clicked on the first slide and began speaking: "Here is a quote from one of the first great works of literature, *The Iliad*, written eight centuries before Christ, in which Homer tells us, 'But when the fire had burned down and the flame was abated, the son of Menoetius scattered the embers and laid there-over the spits, and sprinkled the morsels with *holy* salt.'"

"You see," Christian opened his arms to engage his listeners, "even then, that long ago, salt was honored. Unfortunately, that reverence for salt has been lost over time."

Christian paused for a long second, gazing into the audience. "But not completely." He shook a warning finger. "For many of us—at least subconsciously—salt still flavors our fears." Christian, wearing a microphone on his lapel, stepped away from the podium and stood at the edge of the stage. "How many of you believe that spilling a few grains of salt carries a penalty?"

Several members of the audience raised their hands, smiles on their faces, chatter and giggles in the background.

"More than likely, you've been warned that spilling salt is ominous—bad luck. You then throw a portion of the spilled salt over the left shoulder. Why? Because somewhere, somehow, we've been taught that salt is special, and carelessness begets punishment! Why? What makes salt so dear?"

Christian clicked to another slide showing a mound of decaying meat smothered with flies. "For centuries, decay and rotting were thought to be the work of Satan. When man discovered that salt protected against rotting, he assumed it could also protect against the evil works of the Devil. It followed, then, that Satan himself detested salt, and thus the saying, 'No salt is found in a Witch's kitchen or at a Devil's feast.' Any substance that protected against Satan should, by right, be handled with reverence. To do otherwise, even unintentionally, marked you for retribution."

Christian then took the saltshaker he'd brought with him, unscrewed the top, and shook it to the ground. The audience gave a slight murmur. Christian held up both hands and smiled. "Fear not, my friends; the shaker was empty." The audience buzzed with laughter, followed by applause.

Christian then pulled up the slide of Michelangelo's *Last Supper* and placed the laser beam directly on the overturned saltshaker in front of Christ. "There, you see it, the spilled salt forecasting the pain and suffering Christ was to endure during the Passion. In this painting, Michelangelo through art, punctuates the spilled salt as an omen of bad things to come. Here, the great artist incorporates the symbolism of salt, in a work of art. "So, then, why throw spilled salt over the left shoulder? According to legend, that's exactly where Satan sits; the thrown salt blinds him and prevents him from doing harm to the person who spilled the salt."

Christian then showed a slide of the globe with circles drawn around several locations. "In Pennsylvania, for example, after spilling salt, one should toss a pinch over the left shoulder, then crawl under the table and come out on the opposite side. In Norway, a common belief suggests that one will shed as many tears as may suffice to dissolve the quantity of salt spilled; and a variation of this claims every grain of salt spilled represented a tear to be shed.

Christian then discussed a dozen more popular sayings related to the spilling of salt, ending with: "In some parts of the world the spiller of salt would have to wait outside heaven as many years as there are grains of salt spilled."

When the lecture ended, Christian descended the stage, and was met by a crowed of enthusiastic attendees with questions and anecdotes of their own.

∞

Rupert gently applied cream to the back of his hands in hopes of soothing the unremitting itch. He belched and swallowed the urine-flavored taste. Earlier this morning, he'd taken a medicinal oatmeal bath because the rash had now spread to his back, preventing him from sitting comfortably. Using his small mirror, he examined the blackheads on his forehead, prominent against his pale complexion. He noticed, for the first time, a red tinge to the whites of his eyes. A sign of conjunctivitis—perhaps the special type caused by calcium deposits in the eyes of patients with failing kidneys.

Before leaving for the hospital to work the late shift, he picked up the folder of complaints and reread his notes on Brice. Rupert's face flooded with heat as he remembered how Christian had made excuses for his friend's rude behavior. The anger spread to his neck and shoulders as he recalled the article in the *Daily*. When he closed the folder, Rupert turned his eyes in the direction of his left ear and the Voice whispered, *Why don't you call and tell him how you feel? He called you a psycho.*

∞

Luganos rolled onto his back, his heart pounding, feeling the pleasant dizziness that consumed him in the first seconds after orgasm.

Anna waited until his breathing slowed before gently laying a hand on his thigh. With her other hand, she smoothed back his damp hair, then stroked his eyebrows. Anna kissed his chest. "You never speak of your mother. In that picture"—she pointed to the night table—"your mother has such a kind face."

Luganos smiled and raised one knee. "My mother was a good woman," he said, pulling the sheet up over his shoulders.

"And your father?"

"My father was a complicated man: proud of his heritage, but full of faults. He was seldom home: Africa one month, the Caribbean the next, and then someplace else. Some said he was involved in shady things." Luganos released a deep sigh. "My mother believed there were other women."

"Did she know for certain?"

"There was a photograph. He'd been drinking one night and fell asleep with it in his hand."

"Did it show another woman?"

"More—a woman and child. The picture caused her terrible pain."

"Did you ever see it?"

"My mother gave it to me."

"Then you must have a sibling?"

"Yes, I know."

"Have you ever wondered about him or her?"

"I felt unhappy when I saw the picture, but after time I stopped thinking about them."

"How do you feel now?"

"I don't feel anything."

Anna waited and smiled. "Do you have the picture?"

"Yes."

"May I see it?"

Luganos sat for a moment at the side of the bed in thought. Then he went to his bureau and returned with the picture and handed it to her. Anna looked at it, then looked at Luganos.

"This is the woman?" she said softy. "Oh, my."

Luganos placed two fingers over the woman's lips. "Hush. I don't want to be sad when I'm with you." Anna, well accustomed to pleasing him, laid her head back on the pillow and within seconds drew in a deep breath, responding to the movement of his head, which now rotated between her legs.

28

In India the natives rub salt and wine on the affected part of the body as a cure for scorpion bites, believing that the success of this treatment is due to the supernatural virtue of the salt in scaring away the fiends who caused the pain.

– JAMES M. CAMPBELL

AT THE END of the afternoon clinic, Christian dialed Dr. Jasmine Chang's extension.

"Hey, Jas, Christian here."

"Oh, hi." Jasmine's voice was articulate and breathy as usual.

"I spoke to you about Mr. Pike, the nursing supervisor."

"Oh, yes, sorry I didn't get back to you. We couldn't locate his chart. There were some renovations recently, and we're in chaos at the moment. His group is due for physicals in three months."

"Can you call him in for some blood work?"

"On what grounds? You can't order an employee to take blood test because someone thinks he looks sick."

Christian heard the forced drama in Jasmine's voice and pictured her: designer outfit, wet lipstick, painted nails, and ornate high heels.

"This guy really looked sick—something chronic."

"Maybe, but he has his rights."

"Look, Jas, this is a teaching hospital; you mean we can't ask him to take a few simple tests for his own good?"

"Absolutely not. Unless his performance indicates he's a threat to patient care, I can't get involved. As it stands, we have to wait until he's up for his next physical."

"Can you move him up on the list?"

"The list is already made, and we're booked solid for months."

"Can I peek at his personnel records?"

"Can't do. Would be a HIPPA and union violation; the hospital could get slammed. I shouldn't have to tell you that, Christian."

"Can I call him?"

"You're going to call him and tell him he looks like crap? That's not a good idea. Just remember he's under no obligation to do anything for the next three months. Besides, you might just find the union accusing you of harassing an employee. It wasn't long ago that industries used medical reports to get rid of personnel just to hire someone at a lower salary. At our last staff meeting, Greenberg said to stay clear of any problems with the union at this time."

"I'll be tactful. But I owe it to the guy."

"That's up to you. *Ciao.*"

∞

After hanging up the phone, Dr. Chang narrowed her eyes, worried. What she hadn't told Christian was that she'd opened Pike's chart two days ago and found nothing there: no previous history, no physical examination, no blood tests. She'd looked back at the clinic's calendar, and the last time the chart had been requested was the month she was in Brazil getting her eyelids done. A patient's hospital chart was an official document; this could get ugly, especially if Christian persisted. Dr. Chang felt a wetness in her armpits. Of course, she could blame it on the frequent staff turnovers in the office. Either way, she needed time to reconstruct his chart; any inquiry at this time would definitely be embarrassing to her.

∞

Christian knocked on the outer door to Father Joseph's office. The "Knock First" warning sign fluttered in the strong breeze sweeping through the corridor as he entered.

Mara sat at her desk wearing a mischievous smile, her dark eyes sparkling. "He's expecting you."

Christian searched her face for any warning signs. The cleric's office called and requested his immediate presence. Her smile momentarily took him back to their first meeting in Crystal's apartment. Still smiling, she pointed to Father Joseph's door.

He knocked again and entered the inner office.

"Have a seat, Dr. Christian." The cleric's thin lips transformed into a measured smile. "I see you've become a consultant to New York's finest."

"Not exactly." Christian wondered if this was the reason for the meeting.

"Dr. Greenberg tells me you have an expertise helpful to the authorities."

"That's true."

"May I inquire what?"

"I'm not at liberty to discuss any of the details." Christian noted the unmistakable look of displeasure that passed across the cleric's face.

Father Joseph leaned back in his chair, his gold cuff links, reflecting the light from his desk lamp. A golden crucifix peeked from under his open jacket. He leaned forward on both elbows and interlocked the fingers of his hands.

"Mercy Hospital will close. That's definite." The words reverberated as if spoken in an echo chamber.

"That's bad news." Christian let out an audible sigh.

After a pause, Father Joseph continued. "We've completed our feasibility audit. You and a handful of carefully selected individuals won't be affected. We will assign you to leadership positions in other viable institutions until we build a new eco-friendly hospital very close to this present site. I've not told this to Dr. Greenberg, and I'm asking you—no, *telling* you—not to divulge this information. The full announcement will come at the proper time. Father Joseph paused and nodded slightly, his eyes wide, inviting a response.

"Why are you telling me?"

The priest unfolded his hands and leaned back. "Dr. Christian, whenever an institution closes, an unpleasant atmosphere evolves. Disbelief, anger, and then blame result in unintended consequences. Lawsuits may be filed by the disgruntled, in which case, I may need your help." For a second, the priest's boyish face reminded Christian of a skinny Irish kid he'd played baseball with.

"My help?"

"Yes. You've been identified as a person of stature. I'm asking you not to fan the flames of anger that, God knows, will surely come. We'll need calm voices to discourage the staff from hiring lawyers, or even worse, investigating alleged blunders by the administration. Sides will be drawn, and things will get unpleasant." The priest sat forward, his blue eyes laser beams aimed directly at Christian. "Mercy will close. That's certain. There's no recourse."

Christian's mouth was dry, and his temples were pounding. "You realize this will affect thousands of patients and scores of employees, not to mention the practices of our doctors."

"I do, and that's unfortunate. But the fact remains, the institution is not salvageable."

"There's already talk of poor financial decisions by the higher-ups," Christian said, making no mention of who those higher-ups might be.

"Dr. Christian, be that as it may, I want to emphasize that we'll look favorably upon those who remain calm in the storm. You should seriously consider what I'm telling you."

"I see." Christian cleared his throat and took a deep breath.

"Now, as to you personally"—the priest rubbed both palms together and smiled—"we expect a grant to build the new hospital, which, as I said, will not be far from here. That hospital will continue to serve our diverse population as well as provide a state-of-the-art exclusive private pavilion. It will be generously funded. We will search for a director of medicine, and a handsome financial package will be offered. Based on what I've seen at Mercy, you would be an obvious candidate, and, as chairman of the board, you will have my full endorsement." The priest removed his gold-rimmed glasses and placed them on the desk. "Do you have any questions?"

Christian sat quietly for several seconds, examining the cleric's pale face.

"Not at this time."

"Good, and one last thing: Your involvement with the police has caused me some concern. Should I be concerned?"

"You should not be concerned."

"I'm glad to hear that."

Christian knew the meeting was officially over when Father Joseph reached for a large blueprint and replaced his glasses.

Christian closed the door to Father Joseph's office, and felt the beginnings of a headache coming on. Mara was gone, and that relieved him of any small talk.

He entered the dim hallway and met several maintenance workers. They gave him a loud friendly greeting. Christian could only offer a subdued "hi" in response. He avoided eye contact and faked preoccupation, looking at his watch, while his mind wrestled with the guilt he was feeling. *What will happen to these people?*

Christian felt the conflict of duty. He was close enough to several of the workers to say something. Was he obligated to share the information despite the plea of the priest? By remaining silent, was he committing an ethical sin? If enough people knew the hospital was destined to close, could they begin an uproar to reverse that decision or, at the very least, begin making other plans? Wouldn't that be the right thing to do? But then again, could it be traced back to him? What would happen to him, his job, and the book if he got dragged into a conflict with the administration? Was he the only person the priest had confided in? There must be others; the news was certain to get out. For the present, he decided, he would keep his head down.

Christian took the basement route past the morgue—a path seldom used by most staff because it was dark and spooky. He walked at a fast pace, thinking about his clinic patients and all the people who made the hospital work. *Closing this hospital would be a sin.*

29

*Owing to the importance of salt as a relish, its
Latin name Sal came to be used metaphorically
as signifying a savory mental morsel, and,
in a general sense, wit or sarcasm.*

- ALEXANDER ADAMS

THE PHONE WAS RINGING when he opened the door to his office. He hesitated, momentarily, then decided it might be important.

"Christian speaking."

"You called me a pyscho." Bitterness was buried in the string of words; the muffled voice was spoken through a cloth barrier.

"I beg your pardon?" Christian, still processing his meeting with Father Joseph, had not yet focused completely.

"'Psycho' is an unkind word,'" the voice continued.

Christian thinned his eyes and silently mouthed the word "psycho," His scalp tightened, and his heart rate increased as he realized: *it's him.*

"I agree; but those were not my words. In fact, I never spoke to the press." He waited, listening to the breathing of the caller, trying to construct an image.

"So, you *don't* think I'm a lunatic?"

"I never called you that."

Another long pause followed, interrupted only by a low phlegmy cough. Christian broke the silence.

"Is that why you called? Because you are offended?"

"I *was* offended."

"Are you he?" Christian asked, trying not to sound accusatory.

"What do you think?"

"How can I be certain?"

"You never can be certain."

Christian's mind strained, searching for words to prolong the conversation. "Why?" he asked, his voice more curious than condemning.

"Why what? Why them? Why salt? Come now, Dr. Christian, isn't that why *you've* been called in to figure things out?"

"How do I address you?" Again, silence—just the breathing at the other end. Christian was skilled at listening to breath sounds, the hidden messages from inside the chest: *rales*, the fine crackles heard with heart failure; *rhonchi* and *wheeze*, the continuous harsh tones in bronchitis and the harsher, prolonged *tubular* sounds passing through consolidated tissue with pneumonia; or the short, explosive coughs of anxiety. He heard only the clearing of phlegm and a faint intermittent wheeze from the upper airway of the caller.

"Are you well?" Christian asked.

"What makes you ask that?"

"Your wheeze."

"No, Doctor, I'm fine."

"The last note was intriguing. I'm not familiar with the quotation."

"I'm surprised, Doctor. At the podium you seem to know everything. Don't feel bad; I only recently came upon it myself." Silence followed by a cough and throat clearing.

A chill ran through Christian. *The killer had been at his lectures.*

"Now that you know I didn't insult you, can we talk?" Christian bit his lip, surprised at what he'd just said. He instantly replayed the statement. It sounded bizarre; he was talking to a murderer.

"What?! You are working with the police to catch me."

"That's true. I had no choice but to help. They sought me out." Christian heard the rustle of the caller shifting his position.

"Doctor." A pause. "Do you really think you can catch me? I mean, using your supposed expertise in salt?"

"Yes." Christian knew his response would keep the conversation going; the longer the talk, the more he would learn. *Imagine if I could write this in my book!*

"I mean just you by yourself against me?"

Here was the direct challenge. The killer wanted to engage in a contest. Christian's right leg began to tremble. He felt the dampness on the back of his shirt.

"Yes." Christian immediately wished he hadn't answered. *God, what am I doing?*

"You sound confident."

"Confident that you'll make a mistake."

"Don't count on it, Doctor." Rupert raised his voice, then coughed and cleared his throat.

"Now *you're* sounding confident." Christian heard a small chuckle at the other end.

"Would you care to wager?"

Christian's heart pounded. "Will you stop the killing?"

"Only for the time being. And if you can't catch me, of course, the killings will begin again. There is one condition."

"A condition?"

"You can't tell the police we've spoken. If you do, you'll never hear from me again."

"I can't do that."

"This must be between you and me."

"But I'll continue to assist and advise them. I've given my word."

"Okay, but as I said, this wager is between us. You must find me without telling them we've spoken, and, more importantly, you must use your own resources. Your brain against mine. If not, the killing will continue. Will you swear? Will you swear on a covenant of salt?"

"Yes." Christian's heart was pounding in his chest.

"Then do it now."

"Yes," said Christian, "just a moment." He put down the phone and opened the drawer to a small side table in his office where he kept napkins, sugar, salt, and soy sauce from meal deliveries. He found a small packet and returned to the phone. "I have salt."

"Do you swear?"

Christian placed a few grains of salt on his tongue. "I swear," his legs trembling. "Will you call again?"

"Perhaps."

"I would like to speak with you, to know you; there are questions I'd like to ask you."

"Ah, clever. Something to add to your book, no doubt. But, Doctor"—there was a pause—"you already know me."

The phone went dead. Christian hung up and walked to his bathroom. He splashed his face with water and suppressed the urge to vomit. He shivered and realized his entire body was covered with sweat.

What am I thinking? Agreeing to help catch a killer is one thing but making a covenant with him is something else. But what was the alternative? Lose contact; drive him away? Would it really make a difference if the police knew I'd spoken to him? They'd probably do something to drive him underground, and I would loose the killer and the story. He's smart, but, if I'm lucky, his obsession with salt, the scriptures, and his disease will make him careless; that's how we'll get him; without me breaking the covenant. What a story!

Suddenly, Christian felt overheated—closed in—and needed fresh air. He took the elevator to the roof garden reserved for staff and sat in a shaded chair. No one was there; a soft breeze cooled his face.

Strangely, Christian didn't feel personally threatened. He knew the killer wanted him in the picture, at least for the present. The killer was obsessed with outsmarting him. Christian now felt less guilty about his selfish plan, in fact, he felt justified because he'd stopped the killing, at least for the present.

Keeping Greenberg and Father Joseph happy was key. The last thing he needed was the priest asking him to stay away from the investigation. If he disengaged, the killing would begin again—and he would lose the story.

Christian left his chair and walked to the railing to look at the skyline. Although he felt compelled to join any attempt to save the hospital, he was convinced the fight was futile. He must think of himself, of his relationship with the killer, and what that meant for the book. Given the choice between the hopeless fight for Mercy versus the story and the killer, his decision was clear. For the first time in his life, Christian understood the phrase: "Every man has his price." He wanted this book, and the hospital was now his last priority. And anyway, if he kept his head down as Father had asked, there might be a big job waiting for him on the other side.

Of course, there were still several other problems. What if Greenberg already knew about the hospital closing, and he and the priest were testing Christian's ability to keep a secret? Had the priest offered Greenberg the chief of medicine position at the new hospital for *his* cooperation? These were White men; he was Black. He was definitely at a disadvantage. There was little he could do; he'd have to take his chances.

If it ever surfaced that he'd spoken to the killer without reporting it, he'd be considered an accessory to further crimes committed? It was the killer who demanded the conditions under which the killing would stop: *Do not tell the police!* That was the killer's terms.

The covenant with the killer would stop the killing for the present, but the only way to get more clues depended on his continued killing. Christian would have to find the killer with whatever clues already existed, and that meant reviewing everything that Luganos had in his possession. *If this drama—the murders, the chase, and the catching of the killer could be incorporated in my book, that would be sensational.*

Christian closed his eyes and blew into his closed fist to slow his heart. The killer said they'd already met. Was that true? Over the years, he'd met scores of patients personally in the clinics and in his private practice. He'd also encountered a number of patients when he acted as a mediator for the state and federal government in dispute cases. He couldn't recall seeing a case with salt-losing syndrome in over twenty years. *Thank God it's Friday, and I'm not on call.*

When he called Crystal, she told him she was exhausted and needed a nap, although he was certain he heard muffled moans and sighs in the background.

"I'll call you back," she said and then hung up.

30

Among the Japanese, the mysterious qualities of salt are the source of superstitions. The mistress of the house will not buy it at night, and when purchased in the daytime, a small pinch is thrown into the fire to prevent discord in the family and misfortune.

~ WILLIAM ELLIOT GRIFFIS

CHRISTIAN SLEPT LATE, relieved it was Saturday, and grateful for his bedroom drapes, which allowed only a sliver of sunlight to be traced on the wall near his bed.

He looked at the ceiling and tried to concentrate on the jumble of thoughts streaming through his head. All his life he'd been careful to avoid unnecessary complications, but fewer than ten hours ago, he'd foolishly made a bargain with a serial killer.

Christian sat up abruptly, needing air and sunlight. He skipped his exercise routine, shaved and showered. He dressed in a white shirt, khaki pants, and loafers and left his building. On Fifth Avenue, he turned right at Fourteenth Street and headed for the farmers market at Union Square.

At the entrance to the park, Christian petted a smiling wide-faced American bulldog and placed a five-dollar bill in the bowl of the dog adoption charity.

Just after he entered the park near the subway, he was engulfed by the energy of the place. To his left, an ensemble of Hare Krishnas, relentlessly grinding out a shrill, monotonous raga. To his right, a brigade of Black men sat at chessboards, challenging tourists to sit and match wits. Although it was Saturday, a phalanx of humans poured out of the belly of the subway, like ants fleeing an insecticide. Directly in front of him, a man too grimy to be ethnically identified, and wearing a wool overcoat, scratched frantically under his collar at whatever was tormenting him. In the midst of this commotion, a thin White man dressed in gold short-shorts and a red tank top spun his unicycle in ever-increasing circles while twirling two Chinese ribbons.

At the market, Christian found himself in front of a flower stand. He'd not intended to buy anything, least of all flowers, but the Asian flower seller's exquisite beauty caught him. He stood, momentarily admiring her smile, then handed her the flowers he'd selected. When she handed him the wrapped flowers, their skin touched briefly.

The sun brought out the dazzling colors of the market, but its hot rays forced him to the shade of a large tree. There he stood with a bouquet of flowers in hand, wondering what to do with them. His answer came when a lady with a cart of rags and an old suitcase headed in his direction. At just the right moment, he gave a slight tip of his head, then handed the lady the flowers. As he did so, he heard the unmistakable click of camera shutter.

Christian looked to his side and saw a woman standing just a few feet away, holding a camera. The expression on her face confirmed that she'd been caught in the act. Christian smiled, and the woman, the camera suspended from her shoulder, smiled, raised both hands, and said, "I'm guilty." I hope you don't mind, but I saw it coming," she said. "It was a great shot."

The woman wore a white peasant blouse with several strands of beads and a wide multicolored skirt. Her smile was warm, no makeup, dark hair—maybe an artist, and definitely a tourist.

"Every year, I visit this city, and I'm rewarded with a great photo. I belong to a club back home, and we have an end-of-summer competition for the best vacation picture."

"Do you think that's the winning shot?"

"Of course! What—a handsome man giving flowers to a lady?"

When the woman moved closer, Christian took in her delicate fragrance—a faint mixture of cologne and a vanilla-scented shampoo. Christian smiled. "I haven't any flowers left, but I can offer you an ice pop. I was about to have one myself," he fibbed.

The woman smiled, "That's kind of you."

They walked a few steps to a vendor. The woman with the camera looked to be in her late forties, sophisticated, trim figure, shapely breasts, and no brassiere.

"Not many bag ladies in my hometown."

"We have our share here."

The woman flashed a pleasant smile.

"How long are you visiting?"

She smiled again, this time measured, avoiding his eyes. "Not long."

"Do you often take pictures of strangers?"

"Only when it's a winner. Anyway, you never know what you'll get when you take a picture. Sometimes, I point the camera in a crowd and shoot. Later, I discover something unexpected. I'll tell you a story—this ice pop is delicious, by the way."

The woman smiled, making eye contact, and began to speak: "Three years ago, I stood on this very spot and took a picture of a man and—I presumed—his wife, having an argument. I had a feeling something big was about to happen; it did. I took the shot just as she slapped his face—a once-in-a-lifetime catch. When I got back to Des Moines, I put the pictures in for processing.

"When I picked up the pictures, guess what? The man in the shop was the husband of the woman who owned the photo business, and the girl in the picture was not his wife, but his girlfriend. Worst of all, his wife printed the pictures. You see—you never can tell what you'll get when you take a picture."

"What happened to the happy trio?"

"The wife divorced him, using my picture as evidence in court." The woman licked her ice pop and gave a mischievous smile.

Christian looked away and narrowed his eyes. The thought came to him in a flash. "Yes!" he shouted, then abruptly leaned forward and offered the woman a handshake. "Thank you!"

The woman, taken by surprise, responded with a smile. "Thank you, but I'm not certain I'm deserving."

"You do, indeed! Believe me, you do, but that's a long story. Are you staying in the neighborhood? I'd like to invite you to coffee." He'd wanted to say "dinner," but refrained.

The woman looked directly into his face, then smiled. She reached into a pocket and pulled out a card. She wrote her number on the card and handed it to him, saying, "I'm here for three more days." She shook his hand, making eye contact as they said their goodbyes.

Christian watched her walk away, two thoughts playing in his head: how nice it would be to see those lovely breasts uncovered, and, more importantly, he now had a plan to catch a killer.

31

In the region of Accra, on the coast of Guinea, salt ranks next to gold in value, and according to Mongo Park . . . flavoring one's food with salt, implies the possession of wealth.

– J.J. MANLEY, M.A.

CHRISTIAN DIDN'T SLEEP MUCH during the night, but he woke alert, feeling the adrenaline-like rush he often experienced just before giving a lecture to an eager group of medical students. After breakfast, he called and made the appointment for 11:30 a.m. at the precinct.

When Christian entered Dewey's office, the two detectives were there, drinking coffee.

Luganos rested his cup on Dewey's desk. "Come up with something, Doc?" His sly smile matched the note of sarcasm in his greeting.

"As a matter of fact, I have."

Christian's answer turned Luganos's derisive smile into a frown. Dewey turned on his desk tape recorder and leaned back in his chair. He nodded for Christian to continue.

"As you know, I've given two lectures on salt at The New School."

Luganos looked down at his shoes in a subtle show of annoyance.

"Each lecture averaged two hundred people. It's not unreasonable to assume that the killer attended at least one of these because of the topic. If he reads the paper—and let's assume he does—the story in the *Daily* might have driven him to check me out."

"How does this help us, Doc?" Luganos's face was quizzical, and his right hand picked at his irritated chin.

"I have one more lecture scheduled. And although we don't know who we're looking for, let's take pictures of all the attendees as they enter and, at the same time, try to get an address, or maybe a finger print."

"What?" said Luganos. He leaned his head to the side in frank annoyance. "How on earth are you going to pull that off?"

"The photo should be easy. And if we tell the attendees they'll receive a copy of the three lectures, we may be able to put together an address list, using index cards."

Luganos was silent, and before he could respond, Dewey got up from his desk and said, "I think it has merit. Let's do it."

Luganos gave a prolonged, barely audible sigh.

"Just one other thing," said Christian.

"What?" said Luganos, grudge in his voice.

"I would like to see your files on the victims."

"You think we fucked up, maybe missed something?"

"No, I'm just trying to fill in my picture of our killer."

Luganos looked up at the ceiling and gave another sigh. He then leaned back all the way in his chair and drained the last bit of coffee in his cup. "The files cannot be copied and must remain here at all times. Is that clear?"

"Perfectly."

"This is going to take some time arranging. How much time do I have before your next

talk?" Luganos took out a small note pad.

"Five days."

∞

At 8 p.m. that evening, Crystal called Christian and told him she wanted to talk. When he arrived at her place, she'd prepared a spread of smoked salmon, white fish, Spanish olives, and French bread. Mara was out for the evening.

"I'm glad you came over," she said. "Greenberg and Father Joseph visited the unit just as I was leaving."

"Did they call before coming?"

"No."

"Did they ask for me?"

"No, but I think they were snooping.

"Why do you say that?"

"Just a gut feeling."

"Were there any problems?"

"Of course not. But don't get distracted from your hospital work. Yesterday, Mara hinted there're big changes coming. Don't forget you're a Black man in a White man's world."

"What I'm doing will definitely be good for the book." He reached out and held her chin. "I've given the police a plan to catch a killer."

Crystal took both of Christian's hand into hers. "This book is really important to you, no?"

"Very important."

"Be careful, Christian. I hope it's worth it."

"I think it will be."

"I admire your commitment, but don't get blinded by ambition."

Crystal climbed onto Christian's lap and gave him a deep kiss. "Are you sure I can't make you something stronger to drink?"

"I shouldn't; I won't be able to concentrate."

"Enough serious talk," Crystal straddled him and began unbuttoning her blouse. "Lie back and concentrate on this."

32

*There is nothing more useful for the
human body than salt and sun.*

~ PLINY THE ELDER

DURING THE NIGHT, Rupert felt short of breath while lying flat but comfortable when sitting up. His wheeze was still present, and he frequently had to clear phlegm. The next morning, after a warm shower, his breathing had improved, and he went to work.

Rupert sat in his office and narrowed his eyes, trying to recall the last time he'd seen a doctor. The year before, in personnel health, a physician's assistant reeking of tobacco and coughing incessantly, gave him antibiotics for an earache. At the time they couldn't locate his chart.

His phone rang.

"This is Rupert Pike."

"Mr. Pike, this is Dr. Christian."

Rupert stiffened upon hearing Christian's voice.

"The last time we met, I happened to notice the rash on your hands and wondered whether anyone was looking at it for you."

"Oh, the rash. As a matter of fact, I've been caring for it myself. I think it's due to the latex gloves, but I'm not certain."

The Voice began whispering a medley of obscene words in rapid tempo, making it difficult for Rupert to concentrate.

"I called because the rash looks similar to what we sometimes see in our clinic. In any event, if it doesn't get better, we can find someone to look at it."

"That's kind of you, Dr. Christian; I'll keep that in mind."

"Good. By the way, what have you been doing for it?"

"A little diluted salt-and-water rinse, twice a day."

∞

Christian walked through the doors of the Soho Precinct and felt the gloom of the place.

"I'm Dr. Christian; I believe Detective Luganos left some material for me."

"Oh yeah, Doc." A bored-looking sergeant got up from his desk. "Right this way."

Christian was led to a room at the back of the precinct. He rested his briefcase on a coffee-stained desk, a mixture of plastic and metal, cold to the eye and to the touch, that took up most of the space in the small room. The chair in front of the desk was lopsided, with non-functioning wheels. There were no windows, and the air was a combination of cigarette smoke, stale coffee, and body odor.

Luganos had provided him with the files of each of the murders, minus the autopsy report of the first victim. The four folders were placed in a sagging, lop-sided wire basket.

After two hours and a headache from breathing the stale air, Christian had compiled a working sketch of each victim. He reviewed his notes:

∞

> *M. Gerber: 56-year-old Jewish female with a history of heart disease. She was on a sodium-restricted diet and took heart medication. She lived alone and had no known living relatives.*

The superintendent filled her prescriptions monthly and said she was stingy and very difficult to please. The next-door neighbor said they never spoke. Her doctor said she never quit smoking, despite her disease. The cause of death appeared natural, but in view of the salt found at the scene, her death was likely the work of the killer. She had been recently discharged from Mercy Hospital. The official cause of death was unknown. No autopsy was performed. She was cremated.

G. Rocco: 38-year-old diabetic obese male, non-compliant with respect to diet and medications. His visiting nurse said he ate sweets and watched porn all day, even during her visits. His hygiene was poor, and at times he walked through the house semi-nude, often forgetting to flush the toilet after using it. He had no known relatives or close friends. She saw him twice a month, and she said he was awful to deal with and impossible to please. He was seen at St. Mary's Emergency Room with a toe infection six days prior to his death. He received an injection of antibiotics and a prescription, which he never filled. The official cause of death was secondary to an intravenous injection of a concentrated salt solution.

R. Johnson: 36-year-old Black bisexual male. He smoked marijuana daily and used cocaine regularly. Arrested on two occasions: once for assaulting a male friend and the other for knocking down a drag queen. Known to peddle stolen merchandise. Several relatives in the South said they lost touch with him because of his short temper and intemperate mouth. They said they were sorry he had passed and would pray for his soul. Discharged from Mercy Hospital one week prior to his death. The official cause of death was by a concentrated salt solution, given by intravenous route.

A. Yonkers: 40-year-old White male who lived on pension checks from the US Navy and the FDNY. He was health conscious and took a variety of herbs and special tonics. He smoked pot regularly, according to his neighbors. His apartment was filled with all kinds of medications, including a stash of cocaine and cannabis. The super of the building said he was a con artist. His next-door neighbor said he was a pain in the ass. The official cause of death was by a concentrated salt solution, by intravenous route.

Christian noted that two of the victims had recently been hospitalized and another had been seen in an emergency room. The last victim had no acute medical problems but took a variety of herbs and tonics. He made a mental note to ask Luganos to obtain the hospital charts of the victims. He could still hear Forsyth saying, "If you really want to know what's going on with the patient, read the nurse's notes."

Christian packed his briefcase and walked to the front desk to tell the officer he was leaving. He asked if he could use the men's room, and the sergeant pointed down a corridor. After a few steps, the corridor opened into a large space with one moderately sized office and four stall-like offices with partitions functioning as walls. No one was in the area.

After using the toilet, Christian walked back through the area and noticed the sign on the office door. The nameplate read: Detective A. Luganos. Christian slowed his pace and stood in the doorway. He stepped in. The desk was neat with several folders and books at one end. On the wall behind the desk hung several framed letters. On the right wall there were three photos.

In one of them, a close-up shot, a young Luganos and a man who bore an unmistakable resemblance to him were smiling. Luganos was holding a flag; in the background the Coney Island Ferris wheel was visible.

In another photo, the same man along with two Black men stood surrounded by an array of sponges under a palm tree. Also in the picture, two pretty brown-skinned girls in their late teens stood next to the palm tree. Luganos's father was pointing to one of the girls, whose hand covered her smile, as if he had said something amusing. A barrel with "Bahamas" painted across the front stood amid the array of sponges. Christian left the office, a strange feeling in his head; something in the picture caused him unease, but he didn't know what.

∞

Rupert cleared the phlegm from his throat and spat into a clean tissue. The material was pink: a mixture of mucous and blood. Recently, his gums had become fragile and bled when he brushed his teeth.

Over the years, Rupert had avoided doctors at all costs, having suffered at the hands of technicians and clumsy physicians when getting his blood drawn. But these new symptoms—the nausea, weakness, and blood in his sputum—now forced him to reconsider. Although he suspected his kidneys were failing, he'd vowed never to be stuck again for blood and never, ever, to be hooked up to any machine.

The previous night, as he was drifting to sleep, the Voice had spoken to him: *Why not go and see Christian? Maybe he can help with the rash. It's a win-win: getting help, and, at the same time, spying on the man who's trying to catch you. Goddamn! It could be fun.*

33

One can live without gold, but not without salt.

~ THEODORIC THE GREAT

CHRISTIAN LEFT THE MORNING CLINIC, crossed Seventh Avenue, and entered the hospital. He dialed the number on his vibrating beeper.

"This is Dr. Christian."

"Dr. Christian, this is Rupert Pike."

"Yes, Mr. Pike."

"Call me Rupert." A pause. "Doctor Christian, you offered to look at my rash if it didn't get better. It's not getting better."

"I'm in my clinic today at one; I can see you there."

Christian hung up, surprised by the call. Rupert could easily have gone to personnel health without calling him. Then, again, no one wanted to sit in those uncomfortable chairs with everyone coughing. Christian felt gratified that he'd reached out to Rupert, even though Dr. Chang thought he was being pushy.

The kidney clinic was a madhouse: overbooked and noisy. Over the past three years, all the clinics had deteriorated under the new insurance mandates. When Christian first designed the clinic, the residents saw all new patients. Now, the teaching staff was forced to see half the new cases themselves because of the limited time allotted for each case. The care was good, but there was less time for teaching.

The charge nurse greeted Christian when he entered the clinic and told him Rupert was waiting in room three. She also reminded him that, by clinic rules, hospital staff should only be seen in the personnel health clinic.

Christian knocked and entered the examining room. Rupert, his back to the door, did not turn to greet Christian, but continued to stare out of a window, head tilted to the side, as if in contemplation.

"Mr. Pike," said Christian.

Rupert turned slowly to face Christian. "You may call me Rupert."

Their eyes met. Christian moved to the writing desk. Rupert avoided the patient's chair next to the desk and walked directly to the examining table and sat.

Christian gestured with his hand toward the patient's chair. "We'll get to the rash, but first, a few questions."

Rupert remained seated for several seconds, sighed, then slowly complied.

In answer to a series of questions about his past medical history, Rupert denied having any chronic illness and said the rash was several months old. Christian washed his hands and asked Rupert to sit on the examining table.

His inspection of the rash revealed a dark discoloration of the skin with fresh lines of excoriations, undoubtedly from Rupert's scratching. Several areas looked as if they had recently bled.

"Does it itch?"

"Not often."

This was obviously untrue, as evidenced by the scratch marks.

"It looks as though you've been scratching a lot."

"Sometimes." Rupert's answer was clipped.

Christian noted the sparse subcutaneous fat under Rupert's skin—often a sign of chronic illness. Rupert's fingernails were thin and brittle, and the dark creases of the hands were pale—a sign of anemia. Rupert's lips were pale and sallow.

"How do you feel in general?"

"Fine." The answer was flat.

"Are you ever short of breath?"

"Occasionally, but only when I use the stairs too much."

"Any cough?"

A slight hesitation before he answered. "Yes, lately. I think I have a cold."

Christian gestured for Rupert to remove his shirt, saying, "Let's take a listen to you."

Rupert did not remove his shirt; he opened the first three buttons slowly. Christian noted this reticence and gently placed the stethoscope against Rupert's chest. A faint wheeze was present. After a few seconds, Rupert pulled away from Christian's examination.

"Dr. Christian, what about the rash?"

Rupert's voice was tense. Christian decided not to push things. It was obvious Rupert was not going to cooperate, and, indeed, it would be better to channel this through personnel health.

"The rash doesn't look like an allergic reaction now that I've seen it up close, but I still think it would be wise to get a few blood tests to be certain. In the meantime, we'll get you something to help with the itching."

Christian wrote out the request for the blood tests and a urinalysis while Rupert buttoned his shirt in silent anger.

"You should have these done in personnel health today. Dr. Chang can give you a topical cream or arrange for you to see the dermatologist. I will follow up on these tests with her."

"Must I have blood taken?"

"Yes. Will that be a problem for you?" Christian saw the concern in Rupert's face.

"I have small veins, and it can be painful at times."

"I can draw the blood, myself, if you wish; I'm also anxious about needles."

"No, that won't be necessary." Christian handed the slips of paper to Rupert and said, "We'll get to the bottom of the rash."

Rupert started to leave, then hesitated, as if bringing something to mind. He turned and asked, "How is your friend?"

Christian, still thinking about the rash, took several seconds to respond. "You mean Brice? He's doing well."

Rupert smiled. He had recovered his demeanor now that he was the one who was asking the questions.

"You're very close as I remember?" Rupert smiled again.

"He's like a father to me. He's alone, and his health is failing, but he shops and cooks. He's a very independent."

"He's difficult, isn't he? I remember our ordeal."

Christian did not respond, thinking it was wise to ignore the remark.

"Thank you," said Rupert, then left.

Christian wrote a quick note of his findings, which he would fax to Dr. Chang. Then he dialed personnel health.

"This is Dr. Chang,"

"This is Christian. I just saw Mr. Pike. He's got a suspicious-looking rash. He's anemic but denies any symptoms. I gave him slips for blood tests, and he's on his way over to have them done. I told him you'd have someone look at the rash and give him something for the itch."

"How did he respond?"

"Vague, elusive, even a little angry, but I think he'll cooperate."

"Christian, by right he should be seen in personnel health and not in your clinic. That creates two separate records and lack of good follow up."

"Look, Jas, he called me today. I gave you a chance to see him, and you declined with a poor excuse." He paused. "I've faxed you my findings, and you can add them to his file. I don't plan to see him again here, unless requested."

"Careful, Christian, don't lecture me. If he gets upset, he could make trouble. And, remember—this was your idea."

"Point well taken. I agree he should be followed in personnel health. Call me when the blood results are complete." Christian hung up the phone.

∞

Rupert left the clinic and headed for his office, deliberately bypassing personnel health. Despite his shortness of breath, he walked rapidly, head down, and breathing fast. He stopped in the men's room near his office and vomited.

In his office, he sat, his right leg shaking and his right index finger tapping the desk.

He knows you're sick, the Voice said. *You saw it in his face. He's fucking smarter than you think!*

"Shut up! You told me it was a good idea. I didn't give it enough thought."

I did. Now we know you can't trust him. He said he was going to look at the rash, and out of nowhere, all those bullshit questions and more needles!

Rupert scratched at the rash harder that he had intended. A tiny line of blood oozed from the torn skin. He opened a fresh pack of tissues and dabbed the area until the bleeding stopped. He threw the tissues into his trash basket.

Rupert sat back, his temples pounding. He looked at the stack of mail on his desk and saw the hospital campus newsletter, *Quick Points*. On the front page, there was a full-face shot of Christian with a Sherlock Holmes–style pipe Photoshopped into his mouth. The caption read: "Helping Authorities Catch a Mad Killer."

Look, said the Voice. *It's dated today.*

Quick Points, a mixture of hospital news, cartoons, and workers-of-the-month features, was a creation of the resident staff. Rupert felt a flash of heat in his face as he repeated the words "mad killer." He peered closely at Christian's face, that immaculate white coat, and the stethoscope—the time-honored symbol of knowledge and respect.

That fucking liar, the Voice hissed, and Rupert, half-smiling, agreed with a whispered insult of his own. Rupert listened as the Voice went on: *He said he never called you a psycho—he lied! You know it!*

Rupert left his office and walked to a bank of pay phones in a quiet corridor just off the hospital lobby. He dialed the clinic.

"Christian speaking."

"You lied to me. The Voice again was speaking through a barrier. "You denied calling me a crazy, but you lied. Now you've called me a mad killer."

"I did no such thing."

"No, no, you said it again! I know you did."

"I did not."

"You lied."

"I don't understand. Tell me what you're talking about. We made a solemn pledge."

"The pledge is broken!"

A click confirmed that the killer had hung up.

After the call, Rupert returned to his office and opened up his Bible, searching for a passage of consolation. The Voice was singing in tongues. Suddenly, Rupert's face lit up in a bright grin. He opened the complaint folder and leafed through the names. His smile widened. The Voice, now rapping at breathtaking speed, agreed with Rupert's amazing idea.

∞

The next morning, Rupert woke up with a well-thought-out plan. He knew his blood tests would be abnormal, and that would be a problem. If he chose not to take the tests, he couldn't be certain that Christian would drop the matter. And, although he was under no obligation to agree to the tests, he'd play it safe.

He left the house at 6:45 a.m. and arrived outside of the personnel health office at 7:25. With his administrator's master key, he entered the office and looked up the times the lab picked up blood specimens. There were three pick-ups daily: 10 a.m., 2 p.m., and 4:30 p.m. Next, he located the blood box where the specimens were kept until they were picked up. He then located the blood test request slips and stamped several of them with his nameplate, then wrote in "11:25 a.m." It was common knowledge that food was not allowed in personnel health because it attracted roaches, and that meant the office would be closed between 12:15 and 1:15.

At 12:25, he returned to personnel health and locked the door behind him. He opened the storage box and removed two tubes of blood and a urine specimen whose slips were marked "Pre-Employment Physical." He then replaced the slips with slips bearing his name. He could have easily done the same thing in the general hospital, but almost all of those blood tests would be abnormal. Pre-employment bloods would have a better chance of being normal. By 12:30, he had made the switch, and at 12:31, he was on his way.

∞

At four that afternoon, Christian's phone rang.

"Christian. It's Jas."

"Hi."

"I think you're slipping, buddy. His blood and urine tests are normal."

"What? You must be joking."

"I'm looking at them as we speak."

"Did you see him?"

"No, his blood was drawn by the staff."

"When were they drawn?"

"Earlier today."

"I can't believe it. This guy is sick."

"Do you want his code number to see for yourself?"

"I don't care what it says there; I don't believe it."

"Christian, you've got a problem! Leave this guy alone, or I'll have to get Greenberg involved."

Christian hung up the phone; mystified.

34

All the humors of the animal body: blood, urine, phlegm and the rest contain salt, lest they become corrupted from one movement to another.

~ BLAISE VIGENÈRE

BRICE WAS OUT OF BED EARLY. He had milk and cereal for breakfast and successfully fought back the urge to fry two strips of bacon to go with the slice of toast. At 11 a.m., his phone rang.

"Good morning," Brice said.

"Mr. Brice, this is Peters calling from Mercy Hospital."

"Yes, Mr. Peters?"

"Mr. Brice, while you were in the hospital, you expressed a desire to file a complaint. We have a report submitted by a supervisor that remains open. I'm calling to see if you still want to follow through with that complaint?"

"Ah, Mr. Peters, I do recall being told that I said something to that effect, but I have no memory of it."

"Apparently you did; it's documented. You failed to follow up but did not personally withdraw the request. Apparently, your friend, Dr. Christian, intervened. That was improper. We are required by the state to settle all patient complaints."

"Then let me be very clear, Mr. Peters: I have no desire to make a complaint; therefore, let's consider the matter closed."

"I'm happy to hear that, Mr. Brice, but it's not that simple. In order to close the file, I need a written statement with your signature."

"That's absurd," Brice said, raising his voice. "I didn't file a written complain, and now I have to write something?"

"You see, Mr. Brice, you might have been compromised by medications at the time, and the regulations are put in place to protect your rights. I'm sorry; we don't make the rules."

Brice exhaled slowly. "Well, what do I have to do?"

"We have special forms that are very easy to complete."

"Send me the forms, and I'll complete them."

"We have another problem, and I hope you can us. We're due for an inspection by the State in several days, and your file is the only one out of compliance. We'll try to get you the forms right away. Please complete them as soon as possible."

"Sure."

"Great. I'll make the arrangements and get back to you about when a representative from the hospital can visit."

"Fine. I'll be expecting your call."

"One more thing, Mr. Brice. Dr. Christian should not have withdrawn your complaint. That was a serious violation of hospital policy. Complaints are sensitive issues, and no one can intervene unless specifically stated in an advance directive. Unfortunately, we should have dealt with this before you left the hospital. I know of your friendship with Dr. Christian, and both of us would prefer keeping his name out of the matter. We have decided not to mention this to him and suggest you do the same."

"Mr. Peters, consider the matter closed."

"Thank you, Mr. Brice."

The elevator stopped abruptly, then bumped three times, giving Christian a slight wave of nausea. The old elevators in the School of Nursing were always acting up. The door opened with a loud clang, putting Christian on the fourth floor instead of the seventh, where he'd intended to go. Uncertain of what would happen next, Christian quickly stepped out of the elevator. This wasn't his first experience with this particular elevator, so he decided to take the one across the hall.

As Christian waited, he noticed Rupert's name on the floor's directory. He wondered if Rupert was in his office; he wanted to look into his face again. How could he have been so mistaken about the man's health?

Christian knocked at the office door. No answer. He knocked again, and the door slowly opened—all the doors in the old building had dysfunctional locks.

The office was a small rectangle. A window at the far end provided a scant ray of light; a desk sat against the left wall with a wooden crucifix above it. A small black Bible with gold lettering lay atop the desk. Next to the desk stood an unfinished bookcase with two stacks of journals and a leather-bound photo album. Christian, hesitant yet curious, opened the album. The first page was blank. On the second page was a black-and-white photo of a younger Rupert standing next to a man dressed in white—a nurse or attendant? In the background, an emergency room sign was just out of focus. Rupert, smiling, wore a white hospital gown, a hospital band on his wrist, and the unmistakable look of someone chronically ill. Christian gently closed the album, suddenly overcome with shame: he'd violated this man's privacy.

As he left the office, he noticed a small wooden sign leaning against the desk lamp with the words "Jude: 16" seared into the grain. Next to the Bible lay a copy of *Quick Points*. The phone rang and startled Christian, who inadvertently knocked over a small wastepaper basket at the side of the desk. While the phone continued to ring, Christian bent over to pick up what had spilled out onto the floor. In the basket he saw several bits of tissue paper stained with dried blood and some with dark-red specks as if a bleeding area had been dabbed. He replaced the contents of the basket and repositioned it. He left the office, wondering about the bloodstained tissues and whether he should pursue more information about the sick-looking Rupert Pike. He remembered that Rupert had denied any chronic illness. As he went back to the elevator, he felt ashamed again for having crossed an ethical line by entering Rupert's space. Yet Christian remained confused. How could Rupert's present blood results be perfectly normal given what he'd observed? How far should he pursue the matter? He had already offered help to Rupert, and pushing any further might be inappropriate.

Before going to his scheduled meeting, Christian went to the men's toilet and washed his hands.

35

*In Ali Baba and the forty thieves, the robbers'
plot was discovered when the Captain of
the band refused to eat any salted food for
fear of violating the "Covenant of salt."*

— RICHARD BURTON'S *THOUSAND AND ONE NIGHTS,*
SUPPLEMENTAL NIGHTS

THE EARLY MORNING RAIN brought a cool breeze that freshened Brice's living room. He had taken out his blue summer suit and hung it in the bathroom to smooth out the wrinkles; he would steam iron it later and wear it to Christian's lecture.

After reading the *Daily*, he fell asleep listening to Chopin's nocturnes, dreaming, as he often did these days, about Christian's mother—the only woman he'd ever felt close to, maybe even loved. The affair had been a secret. The marriage between Christian's mother and stepfather had been in decline for years and would have ended in divorce had it not been for his stepfather's stroke. When her husband became totally disabled, Christian's mother decided to stay by his side.

Over the next several years, Christian and Brice drew even closer, so by the time Christian was a senior at NYU, he and Brice had become like father and son. On Sundays, they still often met for a day of music, reveling in Charlie Parker's dexterity or the otherworldliness of Bach's cello suites. After Christian's stepfather's death, they'd become a family, although Brice continued to live on his own. Within two years, Christian's mother was diagnosed with cancer and died shortly after.

Brice had just opened his eyes when his doorbell rang.

"Good morning."

The stranger in the doorway, thin and pale, smiled at Brice. He did not identify himself by name. "I'm from Mercy Hospital with the papers."

"Good morning, please come in," said Brice, always happy to have company. "I'm about to have a cup of tea. Would you join me?"

∞

Dewey sat back and drained the last of his coffee. Luganos, sitting opposite, wore a dark shirt, dark-blue tie, and the light growth of a new beard.

Dewey pulled his chair close to his desk. "Are we ready?"

"As much as we can be," said Luganos, a half-grin on his face.

"What's up with you?"

"I'm fine." Luganos sat up in his chair.

"It's a good plan, and the only shot we've got so far."

"Look, I don't think anything is gonna come of it, but we're ready." Luganos stood up and walked a few paces. "I'm just thinking."

"About what?" Dewey leaned forward with a frown.

"The Doc's a smart guy. Polished, smooth, not what you'd expect."

"What's that supposed to mean?"

Luganos ignored the question. "As I was saying, I was thinking about all angles."

"I know you don't like him, and you don't go for the salt bullshit."

"Okay, but as I said, he knows all that stuff in the Bible, he's giving talks, and he's writing a book on salt."

"So?"

"If we gotta keep everything on the table, you'd agree that the murders are good press for him and his book."

"What are you trying to say?"

"We should keep an eye on him."

"You mean as a suspect?"

Luganos stood up and began picking at his chin. "Look, I'm just saying we gotta look at everything, right?"

"I think the Doc's knowledge can help us get this nut."

"Look, all I'm saying is that we don't let our guard down."

"Right." Dewey slowly nodded his head in approval and watched Luganos leave his office. He couldn't help wondering whether Luganos's critical view of Christian was, in part, ethnically based.

∞

"I can't believe I said those things." Brice shook his head in disbelief.

"You did, and more I was told," Rupert said. He laughed dryly, and then began to cough. Rupert stood up, searching his pockets for a tissue. "I seem to have run out of tissues."

"Let me get you some."

Brice returned from the bathroom with a box of tissues. "I don't remember a thing. Dr. Christian said one of the medicines played tricks with my mind."

"Is that what he said?"

"That's what he told me."

"The tea is very good," said Rupert.

"Would you like me to add more hot water?"

"Please."

When Brice walked into the kitchen, Rupert went directly to Brice's cup. When Brice returned with hot water, his guest was again seated.

"I've read somewhere that Dr. Christian is working with the authorities to catch a mad killer."

"A lunatic is what he is."

Rupert was distracted by the Voice screaming in his left ear, *You see! He did call you a psycho!*

"Do you think he's a lunatic?"

"Without a doubt. But I'm sure they'll catch up with him. Christian's a smart rascal." Brice stopped at his chair, and just before sitting, he wavered and placed his hand to his temple.

"Are you all right?" asked Rupert.

"Just a little dizzy."

Rupert got up from his chair and supported Brice by his elbow. "Then sit and rest."

36

Why dost thou shun salt? that sacred pledge,
Which, once partaken, blunts the sabre's edge
Makes even contending tribes in peace unite,
And hated hosts seem brethren to the site!

~ LORD BYRON

THE LINE FOR CHRISTIAN'S LECTURE was long and noisy. Attendees were allowed into the auditorium single file, each person given an index card requesting name and address with a promise to receive a bound copy of the lectures in return. In keeping with the plan, a hidden camera photographed each attendee as they entered. The cards were numbered and would coincide with the pictures taken.

Christian's lecture featured the symbolism of salt as depicted in art on themes from the Old Testament. He'd chosen *Isaac Blessing Jacob* and *The Return of Esau*, by Raphael and *Lot and his wife in flight* by an artist unknown.

Using the paintings, Christian described how each story depicted salt's relationship to friendship, to wisdom, or to a curse. He ended with the story of Lot's wife, detailing God's anger at Sodom and Gomorrah and how, after being warned by an Angel not to look back, Lot's wife was transformed into a pillar of salt.

At the end of the lecture, Christian met with Luganos and Dewey in the lobby outside the lecture hall.

"Very interesting, Doc," Dewey said with a genuine smile.

"Have you seen Brice?" asked Christian.

"No, was he coming?" said Dewey.

"He said he would. How did things go with the photos and registration cards?"

Luganos looked down at his shoes. When he raised his eyes, he shrugged his shoulders and said, "Let's wait and see, Doc."

∞

Christian arrived home sometime after 11 p.m. He tried Brice again. The phone was busy. On his voicemail was a message from his Aunt Dotty. She was in New York with her most recent boyfriend. They were staying at the Warwick Hotel and would be leaving at noon the next day. She invited Christian to breakfast, leaving him her number and asking him to call her at 8 a.m.

Christian went to bed but a gruesome nightmare woke him during the night. In the dream, the killer stole into his apartment, hid in a closet, and tied him up. He struggled out of the dream just as the killer was stuffing salt up his nose and down his throat—the ghastly punishment inflicted on violators of young girls during medieval times. Throughout the ordeal, the killer sang excerpts from Gounod's *Faust*.

After his morning workout, Christian phoned Dotty and made plans to meet. He hailed a cab outside of his apartment and headed uptown. He'd tried Brice again before leaving the apartment; both times the phone was busy. Christian wondered why Brice, who always wanted to be in on things, hadn't called him yet. He would stop by and see him that night.

∞

"Hello, sugar," Dotty greeted Christian with a robust hug. She had his mother's smile, the same youthfulness, that same countenance—playful and flirtatious. The last time he'd seen her was five years ago. Now, well into her eighties, Dotty was a stunning brown-skinned woman with perfect teeth, lovely hands, and a still-youthful figure. She reminded him of the aging-yet-beautiful Josephine Baker.

"Aunt Dotty—look at you!"

"I'm doing fine, sugar."

"Where's your boyfriend?"

"Sleeping. I wore him out last night," Dotty laughed—part sophisticated and a touch of vulgar.

When they sat, she took hold of his hands and smiled. "Look, sugar, I found this a while ago and thought you should have it." She handed Christian a picture. "It's your mother and father. It was taken in Nassau soon after you were born."

The photo was in sepia and well preserved. The young dark-skinned woman in the picture wore a white dress with white shoes and a wide-brimmed hat. She held a fair-skinned baby in her arms. The man next to her was white and powerfully built. He wore a dark suit and white shirt, open at the neck, a thin gold chain resting on his chest. His mother would have been sixteen at the time; she was full-chested and must have been nursing. His father looked to be in his thirties with dark hair, dark eyes, and a wide grin. He seemed happy and had the look of someone who enjoyed the sun on his face.

Christian sat back, his own heart beating fast, as he studied his father's face. A mystery in his life was being resolved. Seeing his mother and father together in that picture engendered a sense of family he'd never felt, not even after his stepfather entered his life. The man's strong hands held his mother's waist, pulling her close to him. She was smiling and looked happy.

Christian had wondered all his life about his biological father: What did he look like? Was he kind, friendly? His stepfather was none of those things. To be fair, though, his stepfather had given his family name and a safe place in which to grow, but never gave him friendship.

For reasons he could never understand, his mother insisted on telling people that his stepfather was his biological father. The man was dark tan with curly brown hair. Christian was fair and had a totally different look than his stepfather. He was certain that most people suspected that he wasn't his stepfather's blood son. On those occasions, Christian often felt awkward, an outlier, and on display.

Christian looked up from the picture and spoke. "I always wondered why she was so secretive about my real father. She made it clear I was not to ask about him. After she married, it became even more forbidden: she said that asking about my blood father would be an insult to my stepfather. I never understood that."

"Sugar, life was hard in the islands. Your father was always on the move, and there were other women. He was kind to your mother and I believed may loved her, but he was older and White, and she was young and Black and that was the Island. Your mother was embarrassed when she became pregnant, and she seldom left the house until you were born. The other girls often got rid of their mistakes, but she would never have done that." Dotty's expression changed. "There was some gossip."

"Gossip?"

"People said it was rape."

"Well, it *was* rape at her age." He lowered his voice. "Even if he loved her, and she consented, it was rape."

Dotty squeezed both his hands again. "He treated her good after you were born. He always gave money. In fact, he gave us the money to come to the States.

"Was he from Nassau?"

"Oh no, he wasn't from the Island."

Christian nodded. "Thanks, Aunt Dotty." He walked around the table and gave her a hug.

"I must be going," she said.

They hugged again, and he walked her to the elevator. He could see the satisfaction in her face as he put the photo in his breast pocket, next to his heart, and patted it. He kissed her on the cheek and said, "Write to me."

"Sugar, all of this is part of life. And look at you—a big shot doctor in New York City. When I found the picture, I knew it belonged to you. I wanted you to see his face and find peace. I never cared for your stepfather. I knew you took his shit to save her happiness. I know that."

Dotty smiled, kissed him, and entered the elevator.

∞

Christian sat in Central Park and looked at the face of his beautiful mother: her eyes, her soft smile, and her delicate hands. How hard it must have been for a young Black girl to bring a mixed-raced child into that world on that island, where there were few chances for the child to become something. Now, he understood why she married his stepfather. It wasn't love; it was to give her boy a name, make him part of a family, and to give him a chance in the world.

It was true that early on, Christian realized that the marriage was important to his mother. And for that reason, he never spoke of the things his stepfather did to him: the harsh talk when they were alone, the whippings when she was away from the house, and the other acts of meanness—like forcing him eat eggs as soft as snot, knowing that he could hardly swallow them. Or the time his stepfather found soft uneaten eggs in the garbage and made him pick every bit out, put them on a plate and eat them. But the worst was when his stepfather brought home a dog and announced, "All boys should have a dog because it teaches responsibility."

After a month, the dog had become part of the family, but was not yet housebroken. His stepfather blamed Christian and spitefully gave the dog away to a family in the next building, knowing Christian would have to see the dog every day. Thankfully, that family moved shortly after, but that event ended Christian's childhood. He resolved never to expect love or friendship from this stranger, and he vowed to tolerate anything to keep his mother happy. Had she been aware of his stepfather's wrong doings, she would have ended the marriage. Luckily, Brice came into Christian's life and befriended him.

Before leaving the park, he looked at the picture again, carefully examining the man's features. For a brief instance, Christian had the strangest feeling he'd seen this face before. He smiled, knowing it was probably just a subconscious wish to make the face familiar. Or was it?

37

Through you the stench of putrefied flesh is driven away, and the viscera, about to rot by its own filthiness, is preserved for a long, long time by the sprinkling of salt.

~ AMBROSE

THE UNION THEOLOGICAL SEMINARY, located at Morningside Heights, had the best collection of religious literature in New York City. That's where Christian went to answer the lingering questions in his mind since the last murder.

Christian felt certain of two things: the victims were connected, even though, to date, no facts supported that assumption. And the pattern of the murders pointed to the dark side of salt symbolism.

He'd previously told Dewey and Luganos that the urine left at the last murder was just another way of leaving salt. But, leaving urine, a *liquid*, instead of just salt alone, made Christian wonder if there was another explanation. Was the presence of the liquid as important as the salt now?

Christian knew that in ancient times, in both secular and religious ceremonies, urine was used as a substitute for salt. Urine, aside from the body waste products to be expelled, is a mixture of salt and water. Was there something about the liquid that held a particular significance to the killer or to the murders?

Christian was familiar with stories in the Bible using water in rituals of purification, as in Numbers 19:20: "But the man who becomes unclean and does not cleanse himself from sin; that person shall be cut off from the community . . . he has polluted the Sanctuary of Yahweh."

He also knew that early religious worshipers placed basins of water at the temple doors for the washing of hands before entering. Could the urine, then, represent a form of cleansing or even a *distorted* form of, say, baptism—that sacred process of being born again through water? But, if so, why the emphasis on salt in the previous murders? Clearly, salt was *preeminent*, but if water was also important, why not some other way of killing, say drowning?

The liquid confused things and might necessitate a new perspective on everything. Christian hoped that an examination of how salt and water were connected in religious practices or writings might help. At the reference desk, he requested his first source: *The Catholic Encyclopedia*. When seated, he turned directly to the section on baptism, which read:

> Baptism. One of the seven Sacraments of the Christian Church; frequently called the "first sacrament," and the "door of the Sacraments" and the "door to the Church." It is the door of the spiritual life, and by it we are made members of Christ and are incorporated into the Church . . . unless we are born again of water and the Holy Ghost, we cannot enter the kingdom of heaven . . . The result of this sacrament is the remission of all sin original and actual. Water is the necessary matter of the sacrament.

Further on in the section outlining the ceremony of baptism, he found that *originally* in the baptism of the adult, the candidate was required to denounce all the forms of sin formally adhered to. The priest then performed an exorcism, driving out demons or evil spirits before administering the blessed salt.

So, in the adult baptismal ceremony, salt was not part of the baptismal rite, but was administered *pre-baptismally*, for delivering the individual free from corruption and sin.

Christian moved to another source and found a reference to a letter sent from John The Deacon, also known as Pope John I, to the great Senarius stating:

> Salt was at one time involved, but *pre-baptismal* . . . This signifies that, just as all meat is seasoned with salt and is thus preserved, so too the spirit, which by the currents of time has become flabby and waterlogged . . . is seasoned by the salt of wisdom and the salt of the preached word of God.

A footnote in the letter said "see the *Gelasian Sacramentary*," so Christian requested that next. It was one of the earliest documents on baptism that connected the ancient practice of baptism with the present. The text spoke to the Roman ritual of the pre-baptismal rite for giving salt. Two prayers were offered in the section. He examined the first one:

> Almighty and eternal God, Father of your Lord Jesus, look with favor upon these your servants, whom you have called to take their first steps in the faith. Take from them all blindness of the heart. Free them from all the snares of Satan by which they have been held . . . Then, impregnated by the symbol of your wisdom, may they be relieved of the corruption of all desires.

Christian's heart began to race. These were the same words the killer used in his last note: "Then, impregnated by the symbol of your wisdom, may they be relieved of the corruption of all desires."

Christian held his breath and shivered as a chill ran through him. He'd discovered the source of the killer's last note. In trying to understand the meaning of the liquid, he'd stumbled on what the killer was doing: he was cleansing the victims of evil.

This was not baptism, but a ceremony before baptism. It was a salt ritual—a sacred ceremony. Now he was certain that all victims had something in common; something the killer felt was evil.

What did they have in common that required exorcism? Christian took several deep breaths and shifted in his seat. *Each victim had to be reevaluated to find that common thread.*

Christian turned over the document in his hands, noticing it was pristine. The document was obviously seldom requested. *Where did the killer do his research and find the prayer?* He distinctly remembered the killer saying he'd recently come upon it himself. *Could this be where the killer discovered the prayer and formulated his thoughts; maybe sitting in this same chair?* Christian sat for a few seconds to collect his thoughts and blew into his closed fist, the Valsalva maneuver, exciting his vagus nerve and slowing his heart.

Christian approached the librarian at the desk. The man's glasses were oversized and theatrical but were worn with pride. He flashed Christian a wide smile, revealing a small silver bolt in the front third of his agile tongue.

"May I help you?"

"I'm looking at the *Gelasian Sacramentary*. Can you give me a list of other institutions where this document can be found?"

The librarian turned to his computer. After a minute of typing, he looked up at Christian and said, "The listings for a copy like this one are: the Library of Congress, and of course, the original at the Vatican. The New York Public Library may have one online; I'm not sure."

"Do you get many requests for the document?"

The clerk looked at the screen of his computer then looked at Christian. "No," he said flatly.

"Has it been requested in the last month?"

The librarian looked at Christian a long second. "We don't keep that information here, and even if we did, it would be against our privacy policies to divulge it."

"Then there's no way for me to contact the person who last requested it?"

"Not even if your life depended on it." The man smiled again and shook his head in a slow, definite no. He pursed his lips and deftly maneuvered the bolt in his tongue from side to side, then spoke. "Several weeks ago, the FBI was here with a request for information on one of our readers, and we sent them on their way to get a subpoena."

"Is there anyone else I can speak to?"

"My immediate supervisor. He'll be back in two days, but you ain't gonna sweet talk him, honey; he's a Marine."

38

You are the salt of the earth; but if the salt becomes tasteless, how can it be made salty again? It is no longer good for anything, except to be thrown out and trampled underfoot by men.

~ MATTHEW 5:13

THE SMELL WAS FOUL—a sickening meld of feces and vomit. Later, after she had calmed down, Mrs. Palmer recalled the young police officer saying, "Someone must be sick or dead." She remembered seeing several flies buzzing, and how she'd stood in the doorway, calling the superintendent to come see. He told her Brice had passed.

She'd noticed the absence of Brice walking around, and there had been no music the whole day before. This very proper Irish widow had secretly adored her quiet, gentlemanly, and handsome Black neighbor, whose living room was adjacent to her bedroom and whose beautiful music filled her apartment with joy and fantasy.

Everyone in the building knew he'd recently suffered a heart attack. When she saw his newspaper outside his door, she was certain something was wrong. Five years ago, he'd given her the keys to his apartment to accept deliveries. She knew of his recent hospitalization and wanted to check on her neighbor. Now he was dead.

Christian stepped into the misty rain as he left the Seminary. He turned on his cell phone, which had been off since he'd entered the main reading room, and saw the message.

"This is Christian."

"Hi, Doc, this is Dewey. I've got bad news."

"Has he done it again?"

"No. It's Brice."

"Is he all right?"

"They found him this morning. He passed sometime yesterday. We got the call; they knew we were friends. We called you several times."

"Shit, my phone was on silent." A pause. "That's why he didn't show last night. Where is he now?"

"The city morgue."

"The morgue! Why?"

"We couldn't find you, and it was messy. We didn't want to leave him that way."

"What way?"

"He'd soiled himself."

"It must have been his heart."

"What now?" Dewey asked, hesitatingly.

"He didn't want any fuss, no wake; only cremation. I'll notify his lawyer and get started with the arrangements."

39

Abimelech fought against the city . . . and he took the city . . . and he slew the people . . . and sowed it with salt.

- JUDGES 9:45

"BRICE IS DEAD." Christian was sitting in Crystal's living room resting back on her red sofa. "It sounds strange even saying the words."

Crystal placed the cup of tea on the table in front of him. "You said he was your mentor."

"Mentor, best friend, and adopted father. He was a big, gentle man, brown with light eyes, big hands and, of all things, shy. I'm sorry you never met him."

Christian leaned back on a pillow she'd brought from her bedroom. "When I was very young, it was my mother and me, just the two of us. There came a time when I began to wonder about my father. I didn't have a man in my life. When I visited my friends, their fathers seemed strange, almost like intruders. My mother was both mother and father; she was wonderful. There was no lack of love, yet I knew something was different, something was missing. I remember an occasion when a handsome man, fair like me, came to visit. His name was Remy and he was from the Bahamas. He spent the whole day with us: we ate out and walked in a park in Harlem. He held my hand as we walked. I could feel the strength in his hands, yet his touch was gentle. I felt very sad when he said goodbye. I think he kissed my mother as he left. That night I asked her, "Was that my father?" She didn't look at me when she said, "No. He was a friend before I met your father." Christian gave a long sigh and smiled. "I'll take some of that tea."

"Okay, but don't stop; tell me more."

"After meeting Remy, I began wondering what it would be like to have a father. My image of a father, of course, came from the movies. I had no idea my stepfather would be unkind. He was sneaky, but careful not to show his malevolence in my mother's presence.

Then Brice entered my life at a crucial period and saved me. He taught me so much. By the time I was eighteen, he'd introduced me to Bach, Mozart, and Beethoven. He read my term papers in college for grammar. We regularly attended the Frick Museum and the Metropolitan, and he helped me begin my collection of books on African American history. He introduced me to the world of culture and showed me that Blacks were also a part of that world. He gave me books, written by Black scholars, books showing that African sailors visited the Americas, both north and south before Columbus, a fact not taught in schools.

Through him I met Jan Carew, the famous educator, philosopher and expert on the Caribbean. I still have my copy of *Rape of Paradise*, signed by the great writer. Carew wrote extensively on the fate of the Caribbean following the morning of October 12, 1492, the day Columbus stepped on the beach of Guanahani, the day that racism came to the new world.

"What do you have to do now?" Crystal patted Christian's hand.

"Meet with his lawyer, I think. I was his only family, so I'll have make all the arrangements."

"If there's anything I can do, just ask. Do you want me to help with the funeral arrangements?"

"Brice deserves a funeral with his friends saying good things about him, but he didn't want one, so I'll respect his wishes. The only thing I regret is never calling him 'Dad.' He would have liked that."

"Do you want to spend the night?"

"What about Mara?"

"She's asleep. Besides this sofa has a pullout. I can wake you at five. I'll get you a towel and a washrag. We have new toothbrushes in the medicine cabinet."

"Thanks. I didn't want to be alone."

"You're not alone."

"Do you mind if I keep a light on? I have a problem with the dark."

∞

The next two days were busy for Christian arranging for Brice's cremation and his ashes to be sent to the parish in Jamaica where his mother was buried. According to his wishes, all his clothes and furniture would be given to charity after Mrs. Palmer had selected anything she wanted. Brice had also left his piano to the local high school. All his assets, books, and records were given to Christian.

Mrs. Palmer and Christian were sitting in Brice's living room.

"I offered to clean the apartment, but the building super told me they would have a professional company clean and paint," said Mrs. Palmer. "They're going to wait a few weeks before doing anything—it's the beginning of the month, and the rent had been paid, so the apartment legally belongs to you, Dr. Christian, until the end of the month."

"That was kind of you to offer. I'll come back in a few days to look through everything. If there's anything else you would like to keep, just let me know."

"He gave me a key to the apartment. Do you want it?"

"No, please keep it."

40

Cursed is the man who trusts in man . . .
he shall dwell in an uninhabited salt-land.

~ JEREMIAH 17: 5-6

LUGANOS SAT AT HIS DESK sipping black coffee, carefully reviewing the hospital chart of the first victim. He'd requested all the records but, to date, had only received this one. Christian told them the nurse's notes would be helpful. Since Christian was busy dealing with Brice's funeral details, this was the perfect time to get a jump on him.

Luganos wore a dark-blue shirt with a deep maroon tie whose regal color could not conceal the cheap fabric. He had the photos and addresses of those who attended the lecture and would look at those next. He had added the attendee's occupation to the index card. Christian hadn't thought of that, but he did. With all of the information under his control, he hoped to come up with something and stick it to Christian. His phone rang.

"This is Luganos . . . No, I didn't look at it, why? What!"

Two minutes later, Luganos stepped into Dewey's office.

"Now what?" Dewey asked closing a thick folder and standing.

"Trouble."

"What kind of trouble?"

Luganos sat on the edge of his chair and leaned forward. "Do you remember when this shit started, I told the boys in the morgue to take blood samples of all the cases I signed in?"

"I remember."

"You remember I signed in Brice because we were trying to find Christian?"

"Go on."

"The boys in the morgue mistook him for one of our cases and drew a sample of Brice's blood. He was loaded with salt."

"You're shitting me." Dewey sat back in the leather chair. "I'll be goddamned."

41

Among the peasants of the Spanish province of Andalusia, the word "salt" is synonymous with gracefulness and charm of manner, and no more endearing or flattering language can be used in addressing a woman.

~ M.J. SCHLEIDEN

THE LIBRARIAN ON DUTY was a mature, intelligent-looking man with dark-brown tortoiseshell glasses. His face was round, with a receding hairline and heavy eyebrows. He appeared aloof but smiled easily. He had given Christian a document thirty minutes ago.

Christian completed what he was writing and returned to front desk. "My name is Christian—Dr. Christian—and I've been doing research using the *Gelasian Sacramentary*. I requested it again today."

"Yes, I know."

"Are there many requests for this particular document?"

"No, not really."

"Can you tell me exactly how many times it's been requested recently?"

The librarian hesitated briefly, and then began punching keys on his computer.

"Only twice since being in the collection."

"Last week I requested it." Christian showed the librarian his photocopies of the pages. "I was interested in the person who requested it before me."

The librarian tilted his head to the side and smiled. "I can't give you that information. It's against our confidentiality policy."

"May I ask if you were on duty the first time it was requested?"

"Yes."

"Do you recall the person?"

"Somewhat."

"Can you describe the person?"

The librarian leaned back in his chair, but never took his eyes off of Christian. "Why?"

"I'm a physician," Christian said softly. "It's very important."

The librarian gave him another long look. "I do remember the man. A man who was coughing a lot."

"What do you mean?"

"I moonlight as an EMT on weekends, and he was coughing a lot, so I went over to ask if he wanted a glass of water. There's no fountain on this floor, but we have a small water closet in the back. He got indignant and lit into me. Told me to leave him alone."

"Did he copy anything?"

"I can't give you that information." The librarian narrowed his eyes. "You say you're a doctor?"

"Yes," said Christian, handing him his card.

"You say it's important—medically important?"

"Yes, very important."

"Just a minute." The librarian went into a small room and returned. "He requested a number of pages copied. I see you also requested some of the same material. We keep a log of the pages copied for paper inventory."

"Do you recall ever seeing him before?"

"I don't think I should answer any more questions."

"Thank you very much. If you think of anything that might help me locate this person within the regulations of the institution, please call me. It's very important."

The librarian took Christian's card, and then said, "There's something else. Later that evening while I was straightening the chairs, I noticed tissues with dried bloodstains in the wastebasket near his seat. I figured they were his since I'd checked the basket when I started my shift, and it was empty. I didn't touch anything when I emptied the contents into the trash bin. I wiped down the table and chair where he was sitting. Is there anything I should be worried about? Is he infectious? You can't be too careful!"

"No, I don't think so, but you're right; you can't be too careful," Christian replied as he turned and left the room.

∞

"I can't believe the Doc did it. The guy is no killer!" Dewey walked to his window and looked at the street below.

Luganos was happy that Dewey's statement contained at least some element of doubt about Christian's innocence. He rubbed his chin and felt redeemed. He stood, both hands deep in the front pockets of his pants, as if to propose something profound. "You must admit he's a suspect now."

"I agree, but on what grounds?"

"He's a salt expert, he has knowledge of the Bible, and he's writing a book and giving lectures on the subject. More importantly, he's a close friend to the last victim."

"I know it looks bad, but what's the motive here? As for that other stuff, he's a scholar and a writer, and he's doing what scholars do. He and Brice were very close; I know that for a fact."

"Maybe," Luganos sneered. "Maybe too fucking close."

Dewey tapped the windowpane with two fingers. "We don't even have a body now, right?"

"Right," Luganos snapped. "The Doc said Brice didn't want a funeral. Maybe Brice found out something he shouldn't have."

"Let's confront him and take it from there."

42

*Owing to its antiseptic and
preservative qualities, salt was
emblematic of durability and permanence.*

~ ROBERT MEANS LAWRENCE, MD

CHRISTIAN STEPPED INTO SUNSHINE as he left the Seminary, electrified by what he'd discovered. He was getting close and would surely identify the killer—without the help of Luganos. He turned on his cell phone and saw the message. He dialed Luganos.

"This is Christian."

"Hi, Doc."

"I know what he's doing."

"Is that so?" Luganos's voice was sing-song

"I've found the source of his last note. He's doing a ritual—a ceremony to exorcise them. He's cleansing them from some wrongdoing they're guilty of.

"That's very interesting, Doc." Luganos's voice was dismissive. "Look, something has come up. Could you come in now? We have a few questions."

Christian stepped into the taxi, two things clearly evident to him:

Luganos had not listened to a word he'd said, and, for sure, something unpleasant was about to happen.

∞

When Christian entered Dewey's office, he immediately felt a chill.

"Sit down." Luganos's tone was more a command than a request.

Christian had a flashback to his high school days when a guidance counselor had tried to shuttle him into a vocational program instead of an academic track.

Luganos sighed and rubbed his reddened chin. "You recall Brice was taken to the morgue for a brief time. They signed him in under my name, and, mistakenly, assumed he was one of our murder cases."

Luganos leaned over and placed a sheet of paper on the table. Christian looked at the paper, then back at Luganos.

"There must be a mistake."

"I don't think so. The sample was tested multiple times. "

"He murdered Brice." He leaned forward in his chair, placing both hands on the armrests as if he was about to stand up.

"The same day of your lecture." Luganos retrieved the report with care. "Did you visit Brice any time that day?" The detective's voice was bullying.

"No."

"Are you sure?"

Christian looked from Luganos to Dewey. "What are you trying to say?"

Luganos raised both hands, cutting Christian short. "These murders come at a very convenient time, don't you think?"

"Are you fucking nuts?" Christian body stiffened as he leaned forward out of his chair.

"Your book, your lectures? You know what I mean?" Luganos had a sarcastic smile on his face.

"You've got to be crazy to even suggest that." Christian got to his feet. "Brice was a father to me!"

"Would you take a polygraph?" Dewey folded his hands, a soft tone in his voice.

"You mean a lie-detector test? Am I a suspect?"

"Would you, Doc?" interjected Luganos. "All this bullshit about salt—I never bought it. It's too out there. The sort of thing some smart guy would put together." Luganos thrust two fingers straight at Christian. "And we all know you're a very smart guy."

"Fuck you!" Christian, still standing, shifted his athletic frame into a subtle boxer's stance. "You're right, I *am* smart—smarter than you—and when I catch this fucker, it'll be me and you. That's a promise." Christian was dizzy with rage, both his legs trembling.

"Anytime, smart guy." Luganos slowly smiled. He was surprised to see Christian losing his cool and showing a little street.

"Okay, cut it out," Dewey ordered, moving between them. He turned to Christian. "Will you take a polygraph?"

"You're fucking right I'll take your polygraph—with pleasure!" Christian said, looking Luganos up and down.

Dewey sat on the side of his desk. "You said you had something to tell us."

Christian waited a few beats before answering. He could feel his damp shirt and the heat coming from under his collar. He fought to regain his composure.

"I've been trying to sort out a question that's bothered me since the last murder." Christian's voice was now calm, with just a hint of anger. "I was puzzled as to why he'd left the urine. Was he sending a message, maybe a clue? This killer can't act outside the salt theme."

Luganos started to speak, but Christian waved him down. "I believe in this salt bullshit. And I know I'm right."

"Doc, you're full of shit." Luganos poked his head forward at Christian.

"I've spoken to him," Christian said in a low tone.

"You've what?" Dewey's voice was full of disbelief.

"I've spoken to the killer."

"Well, well, well, Doc," Luganos hissed. "You never cease to amaze me."

"Shut up, Luganos." Dewey's voice cut the air as he stood up.

Christian paced away from Dewey's desk. "He called me after the article appeared in the newspaper and challenged me to catch him. He said he would stop killing for the present, but if I told the police about the challenge, I'd never hear from him again, and he would continue to kill. He made me take an oath—a covenant of salt. I had no choice. I knew that stopping the killing was more important than anything else." Christian paused and looked into the distance. "Killing Brice was his way of getting back at me."

Dewey stepped closer to Christian. "Why didn't you speak to us, let us know? Now you've gotten yourself into a big jam."

"I didn't want to take the chance of losing contact, nor did I feel certain that this office could be trusted."

"What the hell does that mean?" Luganos moved within inches of Christian's face.

Christian stood his ground, peering defiantly back at him as he spoke: "I'll remind you of that leak to the *Daily*. Brice told me he was certain it came from this office." Christian's statement was untrue, but he knew there was no way to disprove it.

Luganos stepped back. "You can't prove that." Luganos's face was red, and both hands clenched into tight fists.

Christian turned to Dewey. "I'm telling you the truth."

"What do we do now?" asked Dewey. His body language indicated that he believed Christian.

"He thinks he can outsmart me and the police, and that's how we'll get him."

"This is nuts," said Luganos. "This is bullshit! You can't play this game on us."

Christian moved closer to Luganos. "What do you have otherwise? He's trapped in his own web and can't operate in any other way. I understand what he's doing; he *will* make a mistake."

"You've been a busy bee, haven't you?" Luganos asked.

"He's exorcising them." Christian was careful not to share the information he'd gathered at the Seminary or hint that the killer had been there. He was bent on finding this killer without the help of the police and certainly without the help of Luganos. He wanted to shove the killer down the detective's throat.

"This sounds like more hocus-pocus bullshit," Luganos said, appealing to Dewey with his arms spread apart.

Christian ignored Luganos and spoke directly to Dewey.

"All religions have developed methods of dealing with sin and evil. Every Saturday or Sunday, a rabbi, a priest, or a Muslim holy man calls for defeating the Devil." Christian turned to Luganos. "Do you believe in Christ?"

"What?"

"I asked you, do you believe in Jesus Christ?"

"Yeah." Luganos had planted his feet and squared his shoulders.

"Then, no doubt, you may recall Mark 16:16 that speaks of Christ, saying that he 'casted out demons.' Christ himself empowered the Apostles and his Disciples to cast out demons. I believe our killer feels he's been given that charge. In fact, Christ gave any believer the right to deal with demons and spirits in Luke 9:1 and 10:17."

"Where is this taking us, Doc?" Luganos was breathing heavily.

"Bear with me. Prior to the baptismal ceremony, at one time, adults as well as infants were all exorcised—using salt." Christian looked directly at Luganos. "Were you ever baptized?"

"Don't be funny."

"Then you, too, Detective, have been exorcised. According to Catholic doctrine, infants are born with original sin. In the case of adults, exorcism is needed to renounce the Devil, as well as get rid us of all sins accumulated since birth."

"This is crazy," Luganos said, looking at Dewey, his index finger pointing to his own head.

Christian addressed Luganos directly: "Look, by following my hunches about the salt, I've been able to locate the source of his last note, and now we know what he's doing." Christian raised his right index finger. "I think it's just a matter of time."

"What if he kills again?" asked Dewey.

"He has. He's killed Brice to get to me. He called and said I betrayed him, lied to him, but I didn't; he claimed I broke a pledge. I have no idea what got to him. But he must have known Brice and I were very close. That's important. Brice and I could very well know the killer, or the killer knows each of us separately. But Brice's murder is different from all the others: the killer wanted Brice's death to look like a heart attack. He killed Brice for his own satisfaction and to get back at me. He left no note, no salt, and no urine, unlike the other murders. He didn't want it to look like a murder, and, therefore, he may have been careless, leaving a clue, like a fingerprint that might come up as a match from the index cards." Christian narrowed his eyes. "We have to look at Brice's apartment again and review all that we have on each victim."

∞

Christian left the precinct in deep thought. When he told the police he'd spoken to the killer, he'd broken the salt covenant. And even though the killer hadn't held up his end of the deal, Christian was worried. He had been superstitious all his life, never walking under ladders, careful of black cats crossing his path, breaking mirrors, opening umbrellas indoors, or placing hats on a bed. He'd inherited this from his mother. He thought about the implication of breaking a covenant. Biblically speaking, you don't break a covenant without incurring some kind of consequence—especially a covenant of salt.

Christian was aware of the many times the word "covenant" appeared in the Old Testament, but of the *limited* times the term "covenant of salt" was used—just three. The first was in Numbers 18:19 and dealt with God's covenant with Aaron and his sons, creating the priesthood in perpetuity. God said to Aaron: "All the heaven's offerings of the holy things I have given thee and thy sons and thy daughters, as a due forever: it is a Covenant of Salt forever before The Lord."

The second instance dealt with David and his offspring, when the Lord gave the kingdom of Israel to David by a covenant of salt. And the last reference appears in Leviticus 2:13, when God, through Moses, commanded the people of Israel to be faithful in the offerings of sacrifice, saying: "And every offering of your grain offering you shall season with salt; you shall not allow the salt of the covenant of your God to be lacking from your grain offering. With all your offerings, you shall offer salt."

In each of these instances, God spoke to men, stressing the importance of salt in making the agreement unchangeable and lasting. This worried Christian: he had broken a covenant of salt.

∞

Rupert was quietly wheezing as he entered the Seminary and proceeded directly to the reading room. He requested several items. For the next hour, he took copious notes. After a time, he returned to the desk and requested the *Gelasian Sacramentary*. The clerk at the desk looked at the slip and remarked, "Boy, this must be a hot item."

"How so?" asked Rupert, curious at the clerk's statement.

"Looks like it hasn't been requested for years and then, bingo." The clerk smiled and deftly rolled the contraption in his tongue around the four points of the compass.

"Did you say 'bingo?'" Rupert leaned his head to the side. "I've requested it twice. Have there been other requests?"

The clerk gave Rupert a long look, realizing he must be the person the Black guy was asking about, and his face opened into a whimsical smile.

"Do you remember the other person?" Rupert said softly.

"Funny, that's exactly what the other person asked me about you." The clerk smiled again, mischievously, inviting more questions.

"Can you tell me anything about the other person?"

The clerk smiled again, this time widely, revealing a crooked row of front teeth and his lingual hardware. "He's Black, handsome, and dead serious about finding you. Don't worry, I didn't tell him anything—that's against our policy. He did, however, speak to my supervisor."

"Is your supervisor here?"

"He's here tomorrow. Wait a minute." The librarian got up and headed to the small copy room, saying, over his shoulder: "The man left a card and wanted to contact you. Let me get the card."

When the clerk returned to the desk, Rupert was gone.

43

*Already the fatal day had come; already
everything was prepared for the sacrifice:
the salt and the sacred cakes.*

– VIRGIL, *THE AENEID*

A SINGLE DIM LIGHT hung from Rupert's bathroom ceiling. He lit several candles and sat amid the dancing figures flickering on the walls from the candles' flames. The moving shadows on the rough plaster edged his slight dizziness into a mild vertigo. He coughed, producing only scant phlegm, and frowned at the bitter metallic taste.

He had come to a decision.

In his left ear, he heard the sobbing voices, pleading, in the low cadence of a Negro spiritual. He realized that from the first hour of his cursed life, he'd never enjoyed sustained happiness. His life was always complicated, riddled with pain, distressed, and tortured with chronic infirmity. His mother had often said, "You're just a mess."

The voices were now crying uncontrollably.

His *happiness*, when he dared to think of it, came from the realization that he knew *all* aspects of salt—like no other human. But that gift came at such a price: being born broken and forced, by his need to live, to find the secret of survival. Now, he was tired. It would only be a matter of time.

Rupert stripped naked and lit two additional candles, one cinnamon-scented, the other lavender. He placed two small towels in the face bowl of hot water. He then wrapped his left forearm and left ankle in a towel. Most of the surface veins on his body were already destroyed from the needle sticks during his childhood, but a few, still viable, would dilate from the heat and should be easy to pierce. And even with his great fear of needle punctures, he'd already decided that if no vein could be found, he'd use the large dorsal vein on his penis, which stood out clearly and remained untouched.

Rupert sat on the toilet seat listening to and interpreting the voices; relishing the scent of the candles, he examined the sites under the towels and chose a vein on his left forearm.

Holding his breath, he gently spanked the skin above the vein, unwrapped the thin-gauge needle, and entered the vessel without resistance. Rupert then hung the plastic IV bag containing the salt solution on a shower curtain hook. He connected the IV tubing and started the infusion, watching the cold fluid disappear into his arm, causing a transient chill as it mixed with his blood and vanished into his body. He filled the tub with warm water and stepped in. He sat with his head back to allay his dizziness and waited, knowing that the chemistry inside his brain would soon begin to change. He purposely set a slow rate of infusion so the sucking of water from his brain cells by the concentrated salt would be gradual. The first symptoms would begin in an hour as thirst, dry mouth, and headache; then progress to confusion and coma.

Rupert remembered how salt could revive a drowning fly through its ability to absorb liquid out of any substance. A fly whose breathing tubes were blocked with water could be saved by covering it with salt crystals to suck away the water in the same way Rupert's brain would surrender its water, conforming to the immutable and mystical laws of molecular movement.

∞

Christian called Mrs. Palmar a head of time, and when they arrived they found her waiting at Brice's door. Inside, a dignified stillness was disturbed only by the soft hum of an air purifier. The sun drifted through the lace curtains, layering an orange hue to the living room, now hushed in respectful mourning. They walked through the foyer and stopped in the doorway to the dining room.

Luganos pointed to where Brice had died. "He was sitting there; his face was on the table. He'd vomited and soiled himself. That's why we moved him to the morgue without waiting."

Christian walked to the spot and began examining the floor area.

"No salt was on the table when we found him," said Luganos, derision in his voice.

"Remember, this is still a crime scene," said Dewey, taking a pair of plastic gloves from his pocket and looking at Christian and Mrs. Palmar, "You must not touch anything."

Christian did not miss the sly eye contact between Dewey and Luganos. Christian entered the living room, Dewey headed for the bedroom and study, and Luganos walked toward the bathroom. Mrs. Palmer, wide-eyed after hearing the place was a crime scene, her arms held close to her sides, followed Christian into the living room,

"Mrs. Palmer, did you see any salt on the table where Mr. Brice was found?" asked Christian.

"No, not that I recall."

"Did you see spilled salt anyplace?"

"Heavens, no."

Luganos called out: "I got something here."

Christian walked to the bathroom and saw Luganos pointing into the wastebasket. There, among other trash items, was a dried, crumbled up bloodstained tissue.

"Was Brice bleeding when they found him?" asked Christian.

"No," said Luganos.

Christian recalled what the librarian told him about bloodstained tissues at the Seminary but said nothing. Dewey joined them and inspected the tissues. "The crime boys will want that."

"Did you find anything?" Christian nodded to Dewey.

"Nothing but books, records, more books."

"I'll take a look with you," said Christian.

∞

Thirty minutes had passed since he'd started the infusion; Rupert felt the beginnings of a headache. Could this be an early sign of brain dehydration: the concentrated solution drawing water from his brain cells the same way a gumdrop draws water from a child's inner cheek? It was really too soon for this to be happening. Healthy brain cells are unique among the body's cells; they specifically defended against water loss using old tricks learned over millions of years, as animals faced ever-changing climatic conditions. *His* brain cells were well-accustomed to frequent physiological shifts and would gallantly fight to keep their water content.

He decided his headache was *not* the beginning of symptoms. It was too soon for that. But then, what could it be? *Stress? Indecision? Am I absolutely certain of what I'm doing?* Rupert rested back and closed his eyes.

Suddenly, the Voice shouted, *Stop!*

Rupert opened his eyes. There was agony in the Voice's appeal.

If you do this, he'll certainly win, the Voice demanded. Rupert sat up and leaned forward. His eyes narrowed in concentration, the muscles in his neck tightened, and both fists clenched.

The Voice continued: *Do you want him to be the hero? You'll only be a chapter in his book. Stay alive now and outwit him . . . or take him with you. Yes, kill him first! If he dies, oh, what sweet satisfaction you will have! Call him.*

Rupert gently removed the IV and stepped from the tub and dried himself. He placed a Band-Aid on the site to stop any bleeding. The voice had stopped sobbing and was softly humming joyfully. Before leaving the bathroom, he drank four glasses of water—the amount estimated to dilute the salt he'd received and to replace what had already been extracted from his brain cells.

∞

The three men entered Brice's study—a small converted bedroom. Christian hesitated at the door; his head momentarily flooded with memories of times he'd spent there with Brice. He felt the presence of his old friend as he looked at the books, records, and large gray sofa against the left wall. Above the sofa, he saw the photo of Brice and a much younger Christian, both wearing tennis whites. Brice's powerful arms were around his shoulders, and Christian held a shiny trophy, sporting a big smile.

Brice's desk was on the right side of the study, and on top of it lay a black Bible. Christian looked at the Bible, then turned to Dewey. "Did you put the Bible there?"

"I didn't touch anything. Remember, this is a crime scene. Why?"

"It's strange to find the Bible on his desk."

"Have you seen the Bible before?"

"Yes, in the bookcase. He bought it years ago to look up background info when we listened to Bach's *St. Matthew's Passion*. I've never seen him touch it since then." Christian walked over to the CD player and turntable. The player was empty, and a record of piano selections by Scarlatti sat on the turntable.

Christian turned to Luganos. "Do you have gloves?"

Luganos produced a pair, and Christian carefully examined the Bible without disturbing its position on the table. He pulled the thin maroon ribbon, which opened to a page containing a note in the margin that read, "Indeed, men of God are the salt by which the composition of this world is preserved: and the things of this earth endure as long as salt is not corrupted."

"This is from him," said Christian in a low voice.

Luganos walked over to look at the Bible, then gave Christian an exasperated look. "You said killing Brice was not like the others, that the killer wasn't going to leave anything." Luganos tipped his head once, begging an answer.

"I don't think he left this for us; he left it for himself. He can't help it; he's stuck in his madness. He didn't expect us to discover Brice was murdered, or that we would be here looking for clues. How could he have known that Brice's blood would be tested?"

Luganos took a few steps back, folded his arms across his chest, and smiled again. "Maybe *you* left it, Doc." Luganos's face was now rock hard. "Just in case anyone got suspicious."

"Suspicious of what?"

"That you might be the one we're looking for."

"I didn't kill Brice or anyone else, and you know it."

"It's too bad we don't have a body, Doc. No body; no crime. Remember, you said Brice didn't want a fuss; just cremation."

Dewey held up his hands in a signal to stop the banter. "If you're not the killer, then he's still out there. Could he be after you next, Doc?"

"I don't think so. He wants to prove he's smarter than me. As crazy as it sounds, I think he needs me—at least for the present."

"What do you mean 'for the present'?" Luganos asked.

"I think he'll contact me again to taunt me."

"You sure can predict what the killer's gonna do next, Doc," said Luganos.

"And when he does contact me, you'll be the first to know."

"That better be true, because, by your own admission, we have enough to make your life miserable." Luganos smiled and nodded his head at Christian.

As Christian left the apartment, Dewey was speaking to the forensic team on the phone. Luganos stood in the doorway, a smirk still on his face, and as Christian passed, he pointed a finger in his direction and said, "Be careful; you're not as smart as you think you are."

Crystal smiled as she slid into the booth. Christian felt a mild rush of blood to his face at the feel of her thigh next to his, and the subtle coconut-oil aroma coming from her skin. She'd taken a personal day, and he'd called her to meet him at a bar on Sixth Avenue.

"Brice was murdered."

"What?" Crystal gasped and brought her hands to her mouth.

"Killed by the guy we're trying to catch."

"Why did he kill Brice?"

"To get back at me for calling him 'nuts,' which I didn't. He must have known of our friendship."

"But how?"

"I don't know."

"Are you in danger?" After a pause, "Do you think I'm in danger?" she asked.

"I don't think so." Christian shifted in his seat to look directly at Crystal. "I've spoken to the killer." Christian felt her body tighten and she grabbed his arm.

"You've *what*? Did you tell the police?"

"Yes, but I don't think they believe me—at least Luganos doesn't." Christian looked out the large window by his table. "I'm going to find this guy, because I know things about him that they don't. Soon, I'll tell them who he is and where to find him."

"Christian, are you insane? That's police work. Tell them everything you know, and let them deal with it."

"Luganos thinks I'm the killer, says I'm knocking off people to make my book sell. Can you believe that?"

"That's crazy."

"He thinks I killed Brice. He can't prove it because there's no body. I'm going to stick this killer up his Greek ass."

"Christian, have you've lost your mind?" What are you trying to do?

I know you've spent most of your life trying to prove something, but don't do that now." Crystal shifted her positioned to look him straight in his eyes. "You're not thinking straight. *Does* this have anything to do with that damn book?"

He looked away from the table at the grey sky and the raindrops hitting the window.

"It's complicated, Crystal." Just then, his cell phone rang.

"Christian speaking."

"Dr. Christian, this is Rupert Pike. Please consider this a confidential call. Can you talk?"

"Just a moment." Christian put two fingers to his lips, signaling to Crystal to be quiet. He stood up and walked a few feet from the table.

"Yes, Rupert, I can talk now."

"Dr. Christian, when we spoke in the clinic, I didn't tell you the truth. I am, as you suspected, sick, very sick, and have been for some time. Today, I was unable to go to work because of my illness. I need to talk to someone; I'm not far from the hospital."

"I can meet you in one hour; what's your address?"

When Christian returned to the booth, Crystal asked, "What was that all about?"

"Nothing; some administrator has got himself in trouble and needs advice."

"That's why you had to leave the table?"

"He said it was confidential."

"What's her name, Christian?" Crystal gave him a coy smile and a long sideways look.

"Don't be silly. It's one of our administrators. He said he's sick, and I'm going to meet him in an hour, not far from here."

He gave Crystal a hug, promised to see her later, then left the café. Despite the gloom of the weather, he decided to walk to Second Avenue. The rain had settled into a light drizzle, and a hint of sunshine struggled to peek through a mountain of clouds.

Ordinarily, he wouldn't have agreed to make this visit, but all he could think of was the look that would be on Jasmine Chang's face when she realized he was right, after all. Damn! He knew there was something fishy about the lab test. He couldn't wait to slam it to Jasmine.

Broadway was his favorite street to walk on to lower Manhattan, especially in summer, with its hordes of humans. As always, the street was hectic: people colliding, some gently, some not so gently; everyone curious, excited, on a mission to go someplace or to buy something—sneakers, jeans, shoes, beads, blouses, dresses, cell phones. And the girls—Asian, African, African American, Latinas, Irish, Jewish, and Italian—all stylish and beautiful. He made a left turn, crossed Lafayette, and arrived at the address on Second Avenue.

After entering the building, Christian climbed the two steep flights. The loose iron banister shook in his hand from vibrations of cars slamming into potholes. The poor lighting made him reach out to touch the wall of cold concrete with raised, abrasive edges.

The only lighting came from two dim sconces on each floor and a central cone of muted brightness descending from the top-floor skylight. Dust particles danced in the limited light like miniature fireflies at play. On the second floor, Christian pushed the bell to the apartment. No sound. He pushed the bell again. Still no sound. He knocked once, and suddenly Rupert's face appeared, framed in the doorway, the darkened apartment behind him. The serious expression on Rupert's face assured Christian that helping this man was the right thing to do.

"Do come in, Dr. Christian. I appreciate this on such short notice." Rupert gripped Christian's shoulder with a noticeably tight squeeze.

"Not at all, Rupert. I hope I can help."

The apartment was small: a combined kitchen-living-room area, a bathroom off the kitchen, and a single bedroom in the rear. The stove and refrigerator were faded shades of white, and the floor a dull brown linoleum. A tilted Formica table and two chairs rested as a sad trio against the wall opposite the stove. In the tiny living room, a brown sofa, a small coffee table, and a tan hassock were comfortably squeezed together.

"Please sit—I'm making us tea." Rupert motioned toward the sofa.

"That sounds good," Christian lied, trying to be cordial. He rarely accepted food from any sick person unless he knew the nature of their illness. He decided that tea, at least, had to be boiled; he'd make an exception this time.

Christian sat, surprised at how comfortable the sofa felt, the cushions deep and relaxing. He watched Rupert—frail, thin, and medium height—preparing the tea. Rupert wore no socks, and his jeans, turned up exposing both ankles, revealed that the shoestrings of his thick-soled shoes were double-tied.

In the apartment, the only light came from a moderate-sized window in the kitchen. Rupert mixed the tea on the Formica table then brought both cups to the table in front of the sofa.

Rupert sat, cup in hand, leaning forward, and stared directly into Christian's eyes. The poor light from the window kept one side of his face in shadow. Christian wanted to ask Rupert to turn on another light but didn't.

Rupert sat on the hassock and took a sip of his tea. "I don't take sugar; can I get you some?"

"No, that's fine." Another lie. Christian always took sugar, usually three scoops.

Rupert smiled, took a second sip, and rested his cup on the table.

"As I said earlier, I've been sick for a long time. Since childhood."

"From what?"

"Kidney disease."

Christian sat back in his chair. "I suspected as much when we first met."

"You haven't tried your tea yet, Dr. Christian. Don't let it get too cold. It's a special brew, alleged to have soothing effects on all the organs, but must be taken hot."

Christian paused a long second, then took a sip. *Bitter; I do need sugar.*

"But your test results were normal."

"That wasn't my blood. I substituted someone else's; certain the results would be normal."

The two men stared at each other. Rupert was smiling; Christian was not. Christian felt goose bumps on the back of his neck.

"I see." He stared at Rupert. "You know, that could get you fired, maybe even get your nursing license revoked. I can't help you in that regard. Nor can I keep silent."

"I understand perfectly."

Again, Christian noticed the distinct aftertaste. "I think I will take some sugar after all, if you don't mind."

"Not at all, Dr. Christian." Rupert went to a cabinet above the stove and brought back a small white bowl and a teaspoon. Christian placed two scoops in his tea, stirred, then took a mouthful and rested his cup on the coffee table.

"What type of kidney disease?"

"My problem is salt."

Christian's heart skipped a beat. Rupert's words came out as a declarative sentence, slamming down like a hammer on an anvil. Suddenly, Christian flashed back to the time when, as a teenager, he'd broken his left arm and gashed the left side of his face while showing off at a skating rink. He'd been trying to impress a group of girls, not heeding their caution. He thought, too, of another occasion at the beach, when he'd done a backflip off a railing, also against all warnings, and landed on a three-inch nail that punctured his heel and put him in the hospital for two days.

Christian replayed Rupert's piercing words. He felt a sucking weakness in the middle of his torso. "With salt, did you say?"

Christian's eyelids were suddenly heavy, and his tongue felt as if it were covered with sand. He had difficulty focusing on Rupert's face. "May I use your bathroom?"

"Of course." Christian struggled to lift himself out of the deep cushions. His thigh muscles were stiff, and he stumbled as he started to walk. When he closed the bathroom door, Christian had another flashback to a time when a dentist gave him gas and told him to count backwards from 100. He turned on the cold water, cupped his hands, and splashed his face. He felt along the wall and turned on the light, looked into the mirror, and rubbed his eyes, trying to focus on his face. Instinctively, he opened the medicine cabinet, looking for something, anything. On the bottom shelf, he saw the two bottles. He picked up one and brought it close to his face and read the label: *Egyptian Silk: pure refined sodium chloride.*

Through his increasing fog, he replayed Rupert's words again: "My problem is salt." Christian's legs were giving way, and he tightly gripped both sides of the face bowl. His head drooped, forcing him to look down. He noticed a ball of blood-tinged tissues in the wastebasket.

The door opened, and there was Rupert—pale and smiling. "You see how easy it is to outsmart the expert?"

Christian lunged out to grab Rupert, but all he saw was the blur of Rupert's right hand covered with a white cloth. What followed was unpleasant—the otherworldly odor of chloroform—and, after that, deep darkness.

∞

In his office, Luganos removed his jacket and checked his armpits for body odor. He'd have to dry-clean this suit before wearing it again. Outside, the sun was slipping through gray clouds, and it looked as if the rain would stop.

Luganos sat behind his desk, remembering the worried look on Christian's face as he'd left Brice's apartment. The Doctor was in trouble for withholding information involving a murderer. Luganos chuckled as he thought about Christian's predicament. He wasn't convinced that Christian was the killer, not absolutely. *But you never can tell*, he thought to himself. *Anyone can be a murderer.*

He knew Christian could benefit from the murders with respect to his book, yet he had to admit it *was* hard to picture him killing Brice. But whoever killed Brice knew him well enough to get close.

Luganos remembered Dewey saying, "If the Doc's not guilty, then he may be a target." *Maybe we should put a tail on Christian*, Luganos mused. *At least then we'd know exactly what he's up to.*

Luganos looked at the small rickety table next to his desk and saw the neat pile of index cards, the victim's hospital charts, and Rocco's chart from his emergency room. He now had everything to himself, even the photos from Christian's lecture. He'd need the Doc's help with the photos, but that could wait until he'd gone through everything first. Again, Luganos remembered Christian saying if you want to know what's happening with the patient, read the nurse's notes. Christian made a fuss about the victims having some kind of connection: find that connection, and you've got the killer.

Margaret had been admitted to Mercy. The only non-medical entries were several visits by a nurse/quality-assurance administrator concerning complaints with the room accommodations. An official grievance had been made. The patient had been hospitalized many times in the past and was in the habit of making complaints.

The second victim, Rocco, was seen at St. Mary's Emergency Room and refused to sign out against medical advice. The notes indicated he was going to file a complaint against the hospital's nurse/administrator who had insulted him.

The third victim, Johnson, was a patient at St. Mary's and had caused problems. The night nurse supervisor visited him on two occasions. The patient filed a complaint against the hospital.

Luganos picked up Brice's chart and turned directly to the nursing notes.

"Holy shit!" He leaped from his chair and ran into Dewey's office.

∞

Christian opened his eyes and tried to blink. They were dry—as dry as his mouth. He squinted, but that didn't help. The sting of chloroform was still in his nostrils. He was lying flat on his back on the cold linoleum in Rupert's kitchen. His ankles were bound with duct tape on his bare skin. Both upper arms were tied tightly to his sides with some kind of cord. His lower left arm was secured to his left thigh with duct tape. The lower part of his right arm, below the elbow, had been placed palm-up on an armrest made of folded newspapers and was also tightly secured with duct tape to his right thigh. Above his head, attached to a coat hanger, hung an intravenous plastic bag. Tubing attached to the bag ended in a needle inserted into his right arm. No fluid was running.

Christian blinked again, and Rupert's face came into focus.

"I see you're awake." Rupert was smiling and licking a red ice pop.

"What are you going to do?" Christian's voice was raspy.

"Two things: enjoy this delicious ice pop and then deal with you. You've been searching for me, but, unfortunately, I found you first."

The Voice in Rupert's head sang, *Eeeny, meeny, miney, mo! Catch a sucker by his toe! Goddamn! You really got him! What did I tell you? He didn't have a fucking clue!*

Rupert walked to the sink and washed and dried his hands thoroughly, like a surgeon just before operating. "Before you collapsed, I told you the nature of my disease. You should have seen the look on your face." Rupert smiled.

"A problem with salt," said Christian, his voice stronger. He made a stretching motion with his entire body, but only his head moved.

"Salt-losing syndrome, to be exact." Rupert's voice, razor-sharp, spewed the words with pride.

Christian's body trembled, and the pounding of his heart rocked his head. He pressed his eyes closed, his mind racing, disbelieving what was happening to him.

Luganos's last words boomeranged through his head, echoing loudly: "Be careful, Doctor, you're not as smart as you think you are."

He remembered the frightened look on Crystal's face when he left the café, her words loud in his ears: "Are you insane?"

He thought of the time when he'd been caught stealing a small penknife from Woolworths. The manager had threatened to call his stepfather, who would have skinned him alive, but he'd managed to talk his way out of it. As he walked home that day, his heart thumping in his chest, he vowed never to get in trouble again.

Christian needed time. He had to engage Rupert, get him talking and keep him talking. "What did you give me?"

"Never you mind. It's short-acting and dependable, but don't worry—it's all gone now. I gave you saline to wash out the drug. I want you alert for what comes next."

Rupert did a jig in a circle, and in a singsong voice, rhymed, "You write a book on salt, and whatever you get is all your fault!" Then he rotated his hands in a sanding motion mimicking the slick moves of a rapper. "Do you know how it feels when your salt gets too low? Well, you'll surely know how it feels when it gets too high!"

"I have to empty my bladder," Christian said softly.

"Go right ahead. Isn't saline great? It makes you want to pee. You should know that!" Rupert ended his sentence with a sharp kick to Christian's ribs.

Against his will, and to his utter embarrassment, Christian peed on himself.

Rupert sat in the deep cushions of the brown sofa, leaning forward, the strong pulsations in his neck and temples visible, his face fixed in a grimace.

Despite the pain in his ribs and his wet clothes, Christian needed to keep Rupert talking. "Why did you kill them?"

"Ah, now I see. A few questions, huh? For that book you won't be writing. The answers won't do you much good. But, okay, I'll give you the short version. All of them, in their own shitty way, took health for granted, disrespecting the covenant they'd made with God to care for their body. Remember First Corinthians 3:16-17? 'Do you not know that you're God's temple and that God's spirit dwells in you?' Well, none of them acted as if they did."

Christian started to mention that Brice had done nothing wrong but thought better of it. His back was stiff, and his legs itched from his own cold urine. In a calm voice, he asked Rupert, "How did you choose them?"

Rupert smiled, puckered his lips, and opened his mouth just enough for Christian to see his tongue moving from side to side, red and raw. Rupert dribbled.

"It began with a quality-assurance project to assess patient satisfaction. I wanted to compile a list of complaints and make things better. But what emerged was a group of people who couldn't be pleased, no matter what you did. Eventually it became clear to me what must be done. I had to expunge them of their evil, cleanse their souls, and prepare them to move on."

"What will you do with me?"

"A death, by salt—what else? Oh! That's a great title for a book, don't you think?" Rupert's eyes were now wide, set in a permanent gaze. His movements were quick and fluid, as if he'd gotten a burst of adrenaline. Churned saliva gathered in the corners of his mouth.

"You were eager to find me, query me, and feature me in your book. A whole big chapter, perhaps! Wouldn't that have been a splash? But it won't happen, now. You thought you were smart—the professor who knew everything about salt. I was under your nose the whole time. When they find us, guess what? Two dead men side by side, obsessed and done in by salt."

The Voice in Rupert's head screamed, *Goddamn!*

Christian noted the pulsations in Rupert's neck had increased. But he hadn't started the infusion yet, and that was key. *Keep him occupied with proving how smart he is. Keep him away from the infusion.*

"Rupert, have you forgotten that salt is a symbol of friendship? A person becomes a friend if he consumes a peck of salt with you." *That's not exactly what it says, but it's close enough.* "Didn't we do that, Rupert? Didn't we share salt? Did we not make a covenant—a salt covenant? And as such, haven't we become friends?"

"Yes, we did," Rupert, said, his eyes wide; a dribble of saliva slipped from his mouth, which he quickly wiped away.

The Voice whispered, *Don't let him outsmart you! Tell him what Jeremiah said.*

Rupert smiled and licked his upper and lower lips, then stuck his beefy red tongue in the left corner of his mouth. "Jeremiah said, 'Cursed is the man who trusts in man . . . they shall dwell in an uninhabited salt place.'"

Christian countered: "But Luke said, 'Salt is a good thing,' and Mark consoled us with: 'Have salt in yourselves and have peace with one another.'"

The Voice screamed, *Shut him up! He's trying to confuse you!* Rupert slammed his hand on the table, walked to the IV bag, and started the infusion.

Holy shit! Christian took a deep breath.

Rupert pointed at Christian. "I have won—prevailed—I have fooled all of you!"

The Voice yelled, *Good God Almighty!*

"That's not true," said Christian, spite in his voice.

"What's not true?"

"You haven't won. You kept records, didn't you?"

"Yes, but no one will find them."

"Not true. The police and I knew the victims had something in common. That's what we were looking for." A pause.

"Then you killed Brice."

Rupert stood up from where he sat. "How do you know that?"

"Killing Brice was your mistake. You killed him to get back at me, and that's when you, yes, you, closed the loop. You didn't intend for us to find out that Brice was murdered. You never expected us to test his blood. Yes, Rupert—Brice's blood was tested! Up to that point, you were safe. When we discovered that Brice was murdered, we knew whoever killed Brice had to know both of us and also had to know all the other victims."

He's guessing, The Voice whispered. *I know he's lying through his teeth. Make him prove it. Make him prove he knows you killed Brice.*

"Why would they test Brice's blood?" Rupert gave a forced laugh. "There was no reason to do that! You're guessing at all of this." Rupert hunched his shoulders like a large animal about to pounce.

"No, Rupert, they tested his blood by mistake—a fortuitous error by the coroner's office. Yes, a mistake. You know how fucked up the city is. They make mistakes all the time. Then that got us looking at everything all over again, including all the victims' hospital charts. Two of them had been hospitalized and died by the same method as Brice. Your name is in those charts. It's certainly in Brice's chart, within the nurse's notes. And that's the key. He was murdered the same way as the others. Your name is in each chart and connects you to Brice and all the others and to me.

"So, Rupert, you didn't fool anyone. I discovered that the killer visited the Seminary, and I know he was at Brice's house. There were bloodstained tissues in his bathroom, the same as the ones you left in the Seminary, and the same as in the basket in your office. Am I guessing? No, Rupert, *you* left the note in Brice's Bible. Your plan was not perfect, and you'll die knowing you failed to outsmart anyone! It doesn't matter if you're dead or I'm dead when they find us. You'll die knowing you didn't fool a soul. What you wanted most, you didn't achieve."

The Voice in Rupert's head screamed, *Kill him now!*

Rupert went directly into the bedroom and returned with a syringe. Without looking at Christian and despite Christian's frantic head thrashing, Rupert injected the contents of the syringe into the line in Christian's arm. "This will shut you up."

Time is relative and so are dreams. Christian was surprised by the number of events he could squeeze into the fleeting life of a dream. As he slipped deeper into darkness from the injection, waves or particles—the stuff that dreams are carried on—flashed across his mind as questions: Could this all have been avoided? Should he have declined involvement with the police? Shouldn't he have reported the first time he'd spoken to Rupert? Wasn't it stupid, bargaining with a killer and putting a book above common sense? As he sank deeper, he felt sadness: the book would never be finished, he would not be recognized as a writer, and all of what was happening was *his* fault.

44

The whole land thereof is brimstone, and salt and burning; it is not sown, nor beareth, nor any grass growth therein, like the overthrow of Sodom, and Gomorrah, Admah, and Zeboim, which the Lord overthrew in his anger and his wrath.

~ DEUTERONOMY 29:23

CRYSTAL FINISHED HER COFFEE, left the café, and took a cab to Thirty-Sixth and Eighth Avenue. In the safety of her apartment, she undressed, hoping a shower would calm her. She sat on the neatly made bed and remembered him leaving the café, his movements, distorted by the rain, resembling a shimmering ghost.

Suddenly, she imagined him lying dead, like Brice, murdered. Crystal shivered from a chill. *How did such a cautious a man get into such a mess? And that phone call and him stepping away from the table to hide his conversation; what was that all about?*

Crystal reclined on the bed and felt a passing dizziness. How could she help him? The idea of Christian being in danger and, at the same time, at odds with the police, was too much for her to bear. She closed her eyes and tried to suppress what she was thinking. Should she call Luganos and tell him Christian had information about the killer that he'd kept secret? Wouldn't that be the responsible thing to do? *Of course, it would. But would Christian ever forgive me?*

She had to speak to Christian and tell him what she was going to do. Crystal got up from the bed and picked up her phone and dialed Christian's cell. The call went directly to voice mail. She dialed a second time and left an urgent message.

Crystal's cell phone rang.

"Christian?"

"Miss Deveaux, I'm Detective Luganos from the Sixth Precinct. The dialysis unit gave me your number." The official sound of his voice caused her breathing to catch. *Had something happened to him already?*

Crystal refocused. "Yes, can I help you?" she heard herself say, aware of her trembling voice and tightening in her throat.

"We're trying to locate Dr. Christian. Do you know how to reach him?"

"No," she had spoken the words before she could think.

"Miss Deveaux, this is important."

"Dr. Christian is not a murderer, if that's what you think."

"Do you know how to find him? When did you last speak to him?"

"Earlier today."

"Listen to me carefully, Miss Deveaux: he may be in grave danger."

"Danger? He said he was going to meet someone who needed help."

"Did he say who?"

"He said an administrator from the hospital was sick and needed to speak to him someplace downtown."

∞

The thing that Christian remembered about Champ, the spotted dog he'd once loved, was how Champ woke him in the morning. The dog licked his face and ears. That's who Christian was thinking about when he tried to open his eyes. But that failed, so he relaxed, instead, and returned to dreaming. In the dream, he remembered the first time he'd realized he was a different type of American boy. It was during junior high school, and the softball coach was choosing sides. At the end of the choosing, two would-be players remained: Christian and a blonde kid. Although the coach knew both their names, he said, "We'll take the colored kid—he's fast; you take Jerry."

Champ began licking his face again, and this time Christian opened his eyes. There was Crystal, and right behind her was Luganos, a smirk on his face and a toothpick in his mouth. On the other side of the bed was a young nursing student holding a washrag. She'd been wiping his face and moistening his lips. Next to her was Dewey, a half-grin on his face. Greenberg stood at the foot of the bed.

Luganos, now smiling, was the first to speak: "Remember what I said, Doc? 'You're not as smart as you think you are.'"

"How do you feel?" Greenberg asked him in a half-joking voice.

"Frankly, a little embarrassed."

Crystal squeezed his hand. "Why?"

"I don't have any underwear on, I need to brush my teeth, and everyone is about to give me hell."

"You really should stick to medicine and books, Doc," Dewey said with a serious look on his face. "It's much safer."

"Where's Rupert?" Christian asked.

"Bellevue," said Luganos. "He's being evaluated in the nuthouse before he's charged."

Greenberg spoke again: "What were you thinking when he asked you to meet him?"

"I certainly didn't think he was a killer. He sounded like a man in trouble."

"When did you realize he was the killer?" Luganos asked.

"When he was killing me."

The student nurse left Christian's bedside. Luganos took her place and moved closer to him.

Crystal, sensing there were things the detectives wanted to discuss with Christian, promised she would be back later.

Luganos's phone rang. He stepped away from the bed. He tapped Dewey on the shoulder and they left the room.

Christian looked up at Greenberg. "Anything from the good priest?"

"The place is going to close. He didn't say when, but it's definite. Said he'd find places for us at nearby sister hospitals when the time comes. They're going to build a new hospital and we're part of it.

"What does that mean?"

"He wants us to stay. But fuck that; I've already got something cooking in LA. By the way, he thinks you're some kind of hero, figuring out who the killer was."

"You won't stay for the new hospital?"

"Hell, no, I don't trust the guy. I gotta go; see you later."

Luganos came back into Christian's room alone.

Christian looked up at Luganos. "How did you figure it out?"

"Just as you said, it was all in the nurse's notes."

Luganos gently patted Christian's hand and smiled. "See you soon."

∞

At 8:00 pm, Christian was in a semi-sleep but awoke as Crystal delicately stroked his arm. She rested her hand on his forehead, and he smiled, coming out of his reverie.

"I was so worried. You looked dead when they brought you in. All that salt had affected your head. You were talking nonsense. Some of the things you said were very personal, even slightly vulgar."

"Did I mention your name?"

"Thank heavens, no." She smiled and turned, looking around to see if anyone was nearby.

"The salt had removed all my inhibitions. Now you know how I really think. The good news is they don't think I've lost any function.

"I like how you think; the vulgar part, I mean." She smiled.

"Good. I'm being discharged tomorrow."

"You know I still report to you."

Christian smiled. "I do."

"Good night, professor."

∞

Rupert sat at the foot of the uncomfortable hospital bed. It really wasn't a proper bed—more like a sofa, purposely put there to make the patients feel as if they weren't in a hospital. *They're not fooling me: I'm in a hospital with a disguised hospital bed.*

He had removed his underwear and kicked it into a corner. He was naked. Two rooms down the hall someone was screaming, "Call 911." Farther down, another patient was hollering, "Shut that fool up! He's driving me nuts."

Rupert stood up and looked out the window. It was already dark outside and the light from his night table turned the window into a darkened mirror. He stood sideways and saw his pale body, thin except for his protruding potbelly. He was reminded of the scene in *Taxi Driver* where De Niro says, "You speaking to me."

Rupert scratched the back of his head. "I shouldn't have listen to you."

What do you mean? the Voice said in a low dignified tone. *You almost killed him, didn't you?* You *made the mistake when you killed Brice.*

"Now I'm in trouble."

No, you're not. You are, as of now, mentally impaired from your disease. You'll never go to prison. You'll go to a nice place and do exactly what the doctor's say. They'll have to treat your kidney problem. Who knows, you might even get a transplant. Stranger things have happened.

"I don't want a transplant."

Don't be silly; you want to live; you are survivor.

Rupert walked to the corner of the room, picked up his underwear, smelled the crotch, then put them on. The tight waistband gave him the feeling of security. He sat on the bed, picked up his Bible, and turned to Leviticus.

Epilogue

A certain mystic significance has been attributed to the three letters composing Sal (Latin for salt) . . . S represents two circles united, the sun and the moon. A, for alpha, signifies the beginning of all things; and L is emblematic of something celestial and glorious.

~ ROBERT MEANS LAWRENCE, MD

ONE MONTH AFTER HIS DISCHARGE from the hospital, Christian sat facing Luganos across a table at Yanni's Greek Restaurant. At Luganos's suggestion, they were seated outside under an awning. A pleasant breeze flowed along LaGuardia Place, and pigeons flocked across the street in a small grassy park.

Luganos rubbed his pimple-free chin. "That stuff you gave me worked miracles."

"It was the least I could do after you got me out of that jam."

"Out of that jam? I saved your ass. That creep was about to fry your brain." Luganos raised his hand, got the waiter's attention, and ordered fried squid and ouzo.

"I'm glad you figured things out before it was too late," said Christian.

"Rupert's name was all over the place. Brice was his big mistake. We may never have gotten him if he hadn't killed Brice."

Luganos rested his fork. "Hey, how's the book coming?"

"Everything's in the hands of my editor. I think she feels good about the writing.

"Did you include all the shit that happened with Rupert?"

"I did, and I included a Greek detective who saved my life."

"Then it's going to be a blockbuster." Luganos took a sip of his drink and began eating. He looked up at Christian and smiled.

"What?" Christian asked.

"Where'd you grow up?"

"New York."

"Were you born here?"

"No, I was born in the Caribbean."

"What part?"

"Nassau, Bahamas."

"If you don't mind me asking, I know you're mixed."

"Is that a crime?" Christian smiled.

"It's not. Was your father from New York?"

"Which one? I never knew my blood father. I was raised by my stepfather, who was born in New Orleans."

Luganos finished chewing and rested his fork. "When we brought you to Mercy, I went through your pockets by habit before giving up your personals. I found a photograph of you, your mother and, I presume, your father."

"That's my blood father."

"Your father was a good-looking man."

"Yes, my aunt recently gave me that photo. I'd never seen him before."

"That must have been satisfying for you."

"It was, to some extent."

"What do you mean?"

"Well, sometimes you discover disappointing things about people.

But it doesn't matter, because I didn't know him."

"What did you find out about your old man?" Luganos wore a mixed expression, half-smile, half-frown.

"My mother was fifteen years old when I was born. That makes him a rapist, wouldn't you say?" Luganos's face changed from a smile to a serious frown. He gave a soft whistle. "I guess the old guy wasn't too cool. But, look at it this way—if it hadn't happened, you wouldn't be here."

"That doesn't change the fact that he took advantage of my mother."

Luganos narrowed his eyes, contemplating what Christian had just said. He nodded in agreement. "What you say is true, but that was a long time ago."

Luganos raised up his glass and Christian did likewise.

"Did you learn anything from all of this?" Luganos asked, tilting his head to side.

"I did. You warned me in the apartment—I'm not as smart as I thought I was."

"Hey, you remembered!"

Christian pointed a finger at Luganos. "Did *you* learn anything?"

"I did; I didn't think you could help; I was wrong. Now, I take everything with a 'grain of salt.'" Luganos pulled a piece of paper from his shirt pocket and read: "Let your speech be always with grace, seasoned with salt, that ye may know how to answer every man." He looked up at Christian, smiling. "Colossians 4:6."

They both laughed.

Luganos summoned the waiter, and their glasses were filled again. They toasted, and Luganos leaned in close to the table.

"That wasn't the first time I saw that photograph."

"What photograph?"

"The one you had in your jacket." Luganos picked up his glass and finished the rest of his drink. "Many years ago, my mother showed me a similar photo, probably taken the same day."

"Your mother?"

"Yes, my mother."

"That man in the picture is Drosus Luganos—*my* father."

"What? Are you shitting me?"

"No. I'm telling you we're half-brothers, Doc." Luganos extended his hand across the table to grasp Christian's hand, but in so doing, he tipped over the saltshaker. "Oh, shit! Which shoulder?"

"The left. Satan sits on the left."

Made in the USA
Coppell, TX
19 July 2021